ROOTS
AND
WINGS

ALSO BY MANY LY

Home Is East

ROOTS
AND
WINGS

MANY LY

Delacorte Press

Published by Delacorte Press
an imprint of Random House Children's Books
a division of Random House, Inc.
New York

This is a work of fiction. Names, characters, places, and incidents either are the product of the author's imagination or are used fictitiously. Any resemblance to actual persons, living or dead, events, or locales is entirely coincidental.

Visit us on the Web! www.randomhouse.com/teens
Educators and librarians, for a variety of teaching tools, visit us at
www.randomhouse.com/teachers

Library of Congress Cataloging-in-Publication Data is available upon request.
ISBN 978-0-385-73500-1 (trade)
ISBN 978-0-385-90494-0 (glb)

The text of this book is set in 12-point Minion.
Printed in the United States of America
10 9 8 7 6 5 4 3 2 1
First Edition

Random House Children's Books supports the First Amendment
and celebrates the right to read.

For my grandmother, whose words are gentle and whose strength is unbeatable

ACKNOWLEDGMENTS

Sometimes a thank you is not enough, but you still hope that it is. I would like to thank the team at Random House, including Vikki Sheatsley; my copy editor, Deb Dwyer; and especially my editor, Stephanie Lane: you are brilliant and amazing. My agent, Jodie Rhodes, for believing. Carolyn McDade for writing "Spirit of Life." My friends: Brenda Chambers, Lori Keefer, Maggie Martin, and Jenny Sager, for supporting me; Matt Hackler, for talking shop and for thinking I'm funny; Emily Trentacosta, for being Grace's biggest fan; and Norina Vaira, just for caring so much. Shannon Mischler, Heather Aronson Schatten, and Pat Schuetz, for taking your pens and hearts to the manuscript, over and over. My middle and high school teachers, because the roads you take are often long and you should be thanked for it: Margie (Buchholz) Smith, Jo Ellen Sullivan, Patrick Jennings, and Liane Marshman. Jamie Benjamin, my "best friend." Susan Plovic, my "soul mate." And always, my husband, Danith: fifty years together will never be enough.

Spirit of Life, come unto me.

1

I held Grandma's ashes in a dark wooden urn on my lap. Mom and I were flying her to St. Petersburg, Florida, so she could have a Cambodian funeral and not wander around hungry. I didn't know why an American funeral couldn't do the same thing, but I trusted that my mother knew what she was doing. Next to me and Grandma, Mom sat with her back to me and her face pressed against the window, lost in the endless light blue sky.

The airplane rocked, and I held Grandma tightly to my stomach. Earlier I had tried to place her down near my feet.

"Grace, don't be disrespectful," Mom had scolded. So I put Grandma back on my lap and held her like I might have held a baby.

My grandmother had been only fifty-one years old when she died, so she wasn't an old lady. I had read in a magazine that being in your fifties or even sixties was like being in your forties a long time ago. Whoever wrote that article did not know my grandmother. She had been small and frail, and shorter than I was at fourteen years old. I could have easily put my arms around her waist and picked her up, giving her a shake or two until she started laughing. "Down, Grandchild, down," she would have said as she kicked. But oddly enough, in the urn, she was heavy.

On the plane many passengers looked down at Grandma and me as they walked past our row, but only eight people didn't turn away when I looked back. A couple of them turned their eyes toward my grandmother, like they wanted me to tell them about her death. "You didn't know her," I would have said if they asked. One lady in particular frowned, and her eyes watered. She wanted to say she was sorry for my loss, I could tell. But I didn't want to accept her sympathy.

Mom finally turned away from the window. She had been crying again, her eyes red and swollen, her lips puffy. Considering what her relationship with Grandma had been like, I was shocked by how many tears she had shed in the past two weeks. This was the same woman who was always blaming her mother for everything that happened in her life: *What now? Are you going to tell me how to spend my money, too? When will you ever understand me? Isn't it enough for you that my life is this way?*

My mother was one of those women who spoke perfectly, walked perfectly, and dressed perfectly. Her blouses were always ironed, and the colors she wore went together ideally—never clashing or too matchy-matchy. She was what the cosmetic companies would call a natural beauty. She also had a behind the older boys at school revered. So I'd never understood how "this way" could be all that bad.

Mom wiped her eyes dry and put on her large sunglasses. She sighed. "Up here, it's like we're in a different world. If not for this . . . this plane that holds us back . . . we could, you know, be free and fly."

Like birds? I chose not to say anything, though, and soon the gap between her brows wrinkled in disappointment. It was this kind of moment that reminded me I was not as smart as she was. Or as pretty. Or as perfect.

"You have it so easy. You'll never know what it's like to be caught between two worlds," she said.

"Was it like this, you know, when you came to America?"

Mom returned to the refuge of her window. "No, not at all." I couldn't hear her well, and I took the opportunity to move closer to her, smelling her Calvin Klein Obsession. "I was so scared. I had puked so much on the plane that when it finally landed, I could hardly walk. Your grandma had to carry me off."

I didn't doubt what my mother said. She had never lied to me. If she didn't want me to know the truth, she would just hide it from me. But I couldn't picture Grandma carrying my mother. All of my life, it had been Mom who was strong.

As we approached Tampa International, the captain got on the intercom and welcomed us to the Sunshine

State. He flipped the seat belt light off. The mother in front of me sang to her baby: "We're here, we're finally here," and the kid behind me hollered that he was going to build the biggest sand castle ever. As I held Grandma closer and reached down for my backpack, I was doing everything I could to not jump out of my seat and sing, too: *I am here, I am finally here.*

I didn't know anyone in St. Pete, and Mom would go on record to say that she wished she didn't. But this was where she had grown up. Except for the hurricanes, and the crocodile-infested Everglades, and the fact that it was where she and Grandma had lived when they first came to the United States and where she and my dad had met, I didn't know much else about the Peninsula.

My mother looked away from the small window one last time.

"Don't cry, Mom. You're doing the right thing. Grandma would have wanted this funeral. Remember?" I said.

Two days after Grandma's American funeral, Mom and I drove to Gross's Crematory. The man handed Grandma to my mother in a wooden urn. After staring at Grandma for what seemed like five minutes, my mother said that she would have to drive. So the man reluctantly gave Grandma to me. Her name, Naree Hok, was carved on a silver plate tacked to the lid of the urn. I ran my finger over the nameplate, and found it cool to the touch.

Without speaking, Mom and I took Grandma back to

our car. She told me to put on my seat belt as she did hers, and she adjusted the rearview mirror. But instead of driving off, she sat with the engine running, fists tightened around the steering wheel. Then she started fidgeting with the temperature knob, turning it to the right, then turning it to the left, back and forth. "You'd think they could make this easier," she said, before shutting off the AC completely.

We sat in silence as the heat crawled up our legs and finally wrapped itself around our necks.

Mom hit the dashboard with her fist. "Why can't anything be easy!"

I reached over to roll down our windows. "It's okay."

Tears began to spill, glossing my mother's cheeks, and she rested her forehead on the steering wheel. "I'm afraid."

Even though Mom was only five foot six, she was the teacher at our school who stopped fights between the football players. She was the person at our house who woke Grandma from her nightmares and convinced her that they were in America now, safe and unhurt. So what she had said did not frighten me. I knew she just missed her mother.

I touched the black silk of Mom's dress. "Don't be."

"You don't understand, Grace. I didn't give your grandmother the funeral she asked for," she sobbed.

A funeral is a funeral, I wanted to tell her.

"Now she's going to be stuck here. I don't want her to be stuck here." She pulled out a McDonald's napkin from the glove compartment and blew into it before resting her head on the wheel again.

"No, she won't. She's going to heaven."

"Your grandmother was Cambodian. I didn't give her a Cambodian funeral."

I didn't know what my grandmother's nationality had to do with the afterlife. "Do Cambodians not believe in heaven?"

"You don't know."

She had said it as though there was no hope for me. To a certain degree, she was right. I could look at any girl and tell if she had a cool skin tone or a warm skin tone, but when it came to the important things, I didn't know.

"Well," I said cautiously, bracing myself for the rejection again. "Then you should give her a Cambodian funeral. Then—"

My mother raised her head. "What did you say?"

"You know. We can go to Florida and give her a funeral there. Like she—"

"No, no, no! We're not going there."

"But then maybe she won't be stuck *here*."

Mom's crying abruptly stopped, but her eyelashes were still wet with tears. "Oh."

With new energy I rubbed Grandma like she was a crystal ball. "Yeah. We can do that easily, Mom."

"Well . . . I guess . . . we can go to Florida and give her a Cambodian funeral," she finally said. "We can give her a very nice *bouhn*. Then your grandma will be free from this world, and have a new beginning. She would like that. That *is* the right thing to do, isn't it?"

It didn't take me long to answer. I wasn't sure exactly what my mother was talking about, but it didn't matter.

She could have told me that Grandma was an atheist, or even a Supreme Goddess, and I wouldn't have cared. All that mattered was that the moment I'd been waiting for was about to come. "Yes, yes. It's the right thing to do!"

On the plane, I watched Mom suck on her bottom lip as she held her purse on her thighs. "We're here, Grace. We're here in St. Petersburg. Just like you've always wanted."

"We are." I peered through the small window at the men on the tarmac.

Mom dabbed her nose some more with the wrinkled tissue. I thought that if she could, she would have stayed in her seat and waited for the plane to make a U-turn or something, before flying back to Pittsburgh. And maybe if I were a better daughter, I would have encouraged her to do just that, so she wouldn't cry anymore. But all I could do was think about my scrapbook and the man on the back page of it.

"Well." She laughed softly to herself, and then looked at me in a way she never had before, like she liked me. "I guess you would have to come here sooner or later, huh? I just hope it's all you've hoped for."

The gentleness in her voice took me off guard, so I had to think twice about what she said. I thought back to all the fights we had had about Florida, especially the one on my tenth birthday when I woke up feeling as though I'd grown a foot overnight. In my bedroom I practiced walking back and forth like my mother: upright, with shoulders wide apart, a long neck, head up and focused. I was ten years old. One and zero. Double digits. I felt that I could handle anything.

Until that morning, I had known two things about my father. He and my mother met when they were just eighteen, and they were never married. Except to say that he was "gone," Mom never explained why he wasn't around. But I chose to think it was because they had stopped loving each other. Maybe she was afraid of losing me to him, if he and I spent time together?

I had walked down to our kitchen, and I tapped the middle of Mom's back. She and Grandma were discussing plans for the upcoming summer break. "What's in Florida? Why can't we just go there?" I asked.

Mom turned away from the stove. "Grace, I've already told you. Your dad is not there."

I'd heard the same answer many times, and usually I would walk away, knowing that I would never win an argument with her. But that day I was ten, and I had woken up with a new strength. "I know. But then where is he?"

Mom put her hands on her hips and stared down at me. Her skin flushed with anger, and I was sure that the fire within her would cook her. Yet she asked steadily, "How many times must I tell you that I don't want to talk about it?"

Later, alone, I would come up with several answers. Like, *You have to talk about it. You don't have a choice.* Or, *What are you trying to hide from me that you don't want to talk about?* But at that moment, I answered with the only word that came to me. "Why?"

My mother straightened her already straight posture.

"Grace, you're a kid. Some things you don't need to know. Someday you will, and afterward you'll wish you didn't." She usually spoke like this. She didn't yell very often, but you always felt like she was screaming.

I glared at her. No matter where I was, whenever she was mad I became her student. Never her daughter. *Look at me!* I wanted to holler. *I am more than some kid you grade. I come home with you. I share a bathroom with you. I can hear you when you're sleeping!*

But I couldn't manage to say anything logical. Instead I stomped my feet and cried, "It's not fair! It's not fair! He's my dad!" Grandma tried to grab me from behind, but it was easy to break away from her weak grasp. "It's not fair. I want to see him. You can't keep me from him. He's my dad. He's—"

"Fine," Mom said.

I stared at her in disbelief. Had I really won this fight? I brushed hair out of my face and stood up straight again.

"You want to know?" Mom asked, her face washed of any anger. "Grace, your dad is gone. He's gone. And he is not coming back."

"You've already told me that. Gone where?" *California? Paris? Mars?*

"Just gone. Okay?"

Okay? Her expression was as unmoving and flat as a wall. Like *she* would be okay if someone refused to give her what was rightly hers. My grandmother, after a meal of eggplant parmigiana or pizza or hot dogs, would always return home and head for the rice cooker. "If I don't eat rice, I can't be full," she'd say. I'd never understood that.

She'd eaten as much as I had, and I was stuffed up to my throat. But on that day I did understand. Without knowing my father, I wouldn't ever be full.

"No!" I screamed, until I felt a scorch in the back of my throat. "My dad loves me. Why won't you let him see me?" My mother just stood there and watched me, like I was the star of a freak show. "No! No, it's not okay!" I screamed again before running to my room upstairs.

I could hear her and Grandma talking. My mother's voice grew louder as my grandmother's remained low, which normally happened when the two of them couldn't understand each other, even when they spoke in Cambodian.

I sat on my bed with my knees to my chest, rocking back and forth and eavesdropping. I'd accepted that my mom and my dad had fallen out of love, so in all of my dreams of him, I'd never seen them marrying. Still, she had no right to keep him and me apart. It was not fair that she was in control of everything.

"You let her do anything she wants. What happened when I was growing up, *Mak*? 'Chandra, don't do that,' 'Chandra, don't ask too many questions, you're a kid. . . .' What happened to all of that, *Mak*?" Mom said. From my room I wanted to scream at her, *I'm not spoiled, you're just a witch, a lying witch!*

"Kids now are different. They go to school more, so they know more, and they want to know more. You shouldn't be so harsh with her," Grandma said.

There was a pause, the kind that was heavy with anger.

"What have you told her?" Mom demanded.

"I didn't say anything. Don't worry," Grandma said.

"That's easy for you, because I have to take care of everything."

I shuddered at my grandmother being reprimanded by her daughter. I wondered if she, too, felt like a shriveled grape during these moments. I was furious that my mother was allowed to do this—to suck the juice out of her daughter and mother. *Come on, Grandma, give it back to her,* I thought. *Make her hurt and cry, too.* But as much as I wanted my mother to be in pain, she was right. Even though Grandma was the oldest in the house, Mom was the one who signed checks for bills, bought groceries, set up dentist visits for her mother and me, and gave us money for movies.

There was another pause.

"I told you that we should go back to St. Pete," Grandma said. "Now we're alone. My life is sad. There's no one I can speak to."

"Your life is not sad. Stop saying that," Mom said with annoyance.

"You don't listen. Kids get that way. They get old, and they don't listen to their parents. They do whatever they want. So don't expect different from your daughter." I'd heard this argument many times before, my grandmother sounding pleased each time. "If you'd listened, you would have a husband like everyone else."

It was not unusual for Grandma to speak about how wonderful a Cambodian daughter my mother was, but sometimes, she would remind my mother she was husbandless. And this reminder, a flicker of light, gave me a glimpse of my past: my conception changed everything.

While in my bed that day, I could just imagine my mother standing at the stove, facing the temperature knobs, her lips shut so tight they became white. "I'll take care of it," Mom said.

"How?"

"*Mak*, I know what I'm doing."

"You know everything."

There was another pause.

"That's right, when you need me, it's 'Chandra, you're smart and know things, what do you think I should do?' But when you don't need me, it's 'Chandra, you think you know everything.' You can't have it your way every time, *Mak*."

I fell on my bed and buried my face in my pillow until I couldn't breathe.

A few minutes passed, and I heard Mom walk out of the kitchen and up the stairs, the floorboards creaking under her feet. Every time we had an argument, I would pray that she would come to me, to see if I was okay. But she never did.

I was certain that my dad would have.

Several minutes later Grandma entered the room we shared. Split in half, the room was like a pair of mismatched socks. My colorful side had four posters of Tom Selleck, a man my friends found old and cheesy. They didn't see him the way I did: a strong man, a defender of the weak. I was sure he was a great father to his children. I also had a pink comforter and a large purple trunk. My grand-mother's side was a speckled white. Her bed was covered with a lacy cream comforter, and pillows sewn in frilly shams rested against the headboard. Next to her bed sat a stereo on which she often played Buddhist chants.

When Grandma closed the door behind her, I faced the wall. She was my defender, my supporter; she gave me the comfort that my mother didn't provide. But on that day I couldn't decide who I was madder at, her or my mother. When it came down to it, both of them were the same. Both of them had kept from me what was mine.

Grandma sat on my bed and rubbed my back. She smelled of lemon-scented Joy. "Mom love you," she said.

I moved my head onto her lap and thought about how my mother hated her life, how maybe on some nights she hated me, too. Maybe I was part of why her life is this way. "No, she doesn't," I said. Because of her poor understanding of English, I had to speak Cambodian.

"Don't say that," Grandma said. She often defended Mom.

"I want to see my dad. What does he look like?"

She shrugged like a little kid who didn't know any-thing, instead of a grandmother who was supposed to know everything.

"Did he ever see me when I was a baby?" I whimpered into her stomach. What I really wanted to know was if he had ever held me. I wondered if it would be different to have a man hold you. I'd seen Tom Selleck holding a baby once. From the way he cradled her against his chest, you'd think he would crush her. It was so comforting and confusing to see that tiny baby in his arms that I had felt I would die if I didn't know what it would feel like to be that baby girl. "I hate her. I'm going to pack everything in your old green suitcase and run away."

She breathed deeply. "Where would you go?"

"You know where," I said. But after thinking about it, I decided against assuming that she was smart enough to know what I meant. "I want to find my dad."

She took her hands off me and sat still, hunched.

I loved my grandmother. But until then I hadn't considered taking her with me. I wouldn't have been able to care for her the way Mom did. But I didn't want to hurt her feelings. "You can come, too. We can run away together, Grandma."

"Grrr-eh!" she exclaimed and pushed me up from her lap. The force of her voice surprised me, and I hit my head on the wall. It was the first time I could remember her ever raising her voice at me. "You can't say that. Do you hear me?"

I kept my head low. "You want to go to St. Pete, too. Why can't we just go there?"

"Our family is small. We can't separate. So don't ever talk about leaving your mom. It's sinful."

"*Chas.*" I stared at the wall, and we stayed in silence until I mumbled, "You don't understand."

She didn't respond, but in that silence I heard more from her than I had expected to.

Maybe she understood that I hadn't drawn my family tree in the second grade, that I had taken an "I" for incomplete just so I wouldn't have to show-and-tell about my family. Maybe she also understood that everybody at school had moms and dads, brothers and sisters, and aunts and uncles. Their lives connected to each other like a road map. Ours connected to no one. We were three dead ends.

Grandma pulled me to her fragile body. Then she stood up, looked at me carefully, and walked to her bed, tucking her hand under the mattress until she found something. She returned and handed me a white envelope.

"What is it?"

She put a finger on her lips and whispered, "Open it."

It was a black-and-white three-by-five picture with fingerprints smudged all around the edges. I didn't have to ask her who the dark-skinned man in the photograph was.

"Don't tell your mother, Grandchild. Do you hear me?"

"Chas," I said.

"It's the only picture I have of your father. I'll keep it safe for you until you're older."

I traced my dad's solemn face, noticing that his chin was pointy like mine, and that his smile revealed a row of slightly crooked teeth. His eyes narrowed inward like lopsided pears. It could have been my imagination, but I was sure he was looking at me.

Grandma kissed the top of my head. Then she took the picture and put it back under her mattress.

After that day, my grandmother never shared the photo with me again. And when I asked about it, she said she didn't know what I was talking about, that she didn't even know who my father was. But I was certain she was wrong, certain that she was just confused. Many times I snuck a peek at the picture when she wasn't around. But the morning after her death, after Mr. Grubbs and his assistant drove her away, I dug my hand under her mattress and grabbed the picture. And for the next couple of nights, I slept with it under my pillow, so grateful that for one day, my grandmother had been well enough to understand the importance of knowing who your father was.

2

Until Mom finished college and could save enough money, we lived in a cramped apartment near the two universities in the city of Pittsburgh. Grandma stayed home with me while my mother was at school or at her full-time job. I was five when Mom got her teaching job, and we made the move to Scottsville, Pennsylvania, a small town that had two elementary schools, a combined middle and high school, a Wal-Mart, and a Burger King.

It was quiet in Scottsville, and Grandma complained that there were no other Asians. In the city, we hadn't known any Cambodians, but at least we saw other people with black hair who didn't look American. Grandma asked Mom why she had to pick a place so far away from grocery stores. "No *Azi* store here, only *Americ,*" she said. Mom answered that a fifty-minute drive into Pittsburgh was not far.

I found our new house pretty, but Grandma didn't. She thought it was too small, without enough land, unlike her old house in Florida. There wouldn't be room in the backyard for a mango or longan tree, and she would have to grow lemongrass in a large pot on the front porch and bring it into the garage during the winter. She also complained about the paint colors that Mom had chosen for the living room. The walls were dark blue, the shade of the sky near nighttime. When my mother had brought the paint cans home, I had been sitting in a corner.

"White walls make a house look big and clean. These colors," Grandma had said, pointing to the paint cans, "make it like a clown's house."

My mother scanned the room that she had prepared with masking tape and plastic sheets. "It's my house," she said.

"Everybody knows this is your house." Grandma dropped the paint roller and walked up the narrow stairway to our room. I was glad to see her leave, because it meant that she and Mom would not argue.

While Mom stared out the window, her gaze stuck on a bee circling a fully blossomed rose, I wished for my father. Even though I was only five, I knew that as an Asian man, he wouldn't be as broad-shouldered or tall as Tom Selleck. But I was certain that he would be as strong. With him around, my grandmother would no longer remind my mother that she was husbandless. With him around, my mother might have painted the house pink or yellow, her favorite color, and not a sad blue. And maybe, too, she might not look at me sometimes like she blamed me for her life. We would all be happier with him around.

Mom turned to me. "What about you? You don't like it either, do you?"

Before I could say that I did, that I liked everything she picked out, she told me to go to my grandmother and make sure she was okay.

Above the sofa in our living room hung a picture of the three of us. Mom had hired a photographer to take it not long after we moved in. And after she put it up, Grandma quit complaining about the blue walls. For a small space, the picture and the gold frame around it were huge, measuring about three feet by four, so no one could miss seeing us as a family when they entered our house.

In the photograph, we were so chic we could pose for the cover of a magazine. Mom had had us wear similar colors: white pants and yellow tops. Early that morning, she had washed my hair and brushed it dry before tying it in pigtails. Then she had blow-dried Grandma's perm loose and applied neutral colors of eye shadow and blush. Afterward my grandmother and I had sat watching *Magnum P.I.* while Mom got herself ready.

My mother's eyes were tiny and narrow, but the dimples on either side of her mouth made up for them. I had inherited her dimples. She was tall and thin, not petite like Grandma or the other Asian women in the city. Grandma said that Mom was proportioned like *Americ* because she consumed so much milk and other dairy products when they first came to the U.S.

Still, when Mom brought home the picture, it wasn't her image that caught my eye. Nor was it my own, even though, at five years old, I couldn't help looking adorable. I stared instead at the likeness of my grandmother.

As the three of us stood in the middle of the living room and gazed at the large photograph, I pointed. "Mom, look at Grandma's face." The cheek that was melted-looking and discolored no longer seemed to be tugging at her eye and the corner of her lips. In the picture her cheek was as smooth as if it had been stretched and pulled and the excess skin trimmed off, and her entire face was one color, roasted almond. She looked more beautiful than she ever had in real life.

Mom squeezed my shoulder, and I quickly stopped pointing. Like the scar on my grandma's belly, the scar on her face was something the three of us did not talk about. The one time I tried to ask about the burn on her cheek, Grandma held her hands to her ears and started screaming—the sound seeming louder than what our house could hold. I thought she was hurt. A knife from nowhere thrown at her! Or her insides all torn up! I felt light all over, as though no bone was holding me up. And I screamed, too, until Mom shoved me into a corner and ordered me to be quiet. From there, I watched my grandmother shuffling back and forth between the kitchen and living room, and my mother walking beside her, stroking her back and telling her that everything was all right.

Grandma didn't seem to have heard what I said about her face in the photograph, though. She was in her own bubble of happiness. She dragged a chair from the dining table and placed it in front of the sofa, where she sat for the next hour.

In the following weeks and months, Grandma and I stared at that photograph together. When I grew older, as my grandmother continued to marvel at herself, I began to see the large picture differently. I saw that the painted canvas was not complete, that there was a vacancy. Similar to the one in my heart, it was a vacancy that neither my mother nor grandmother could fill.

The night before Grandma's American funeral service, Mom pulled out packages of beef and chicken breasts from the freezer, and tomatoes, bok choy, green onions, and spinach from the refrigerator, lining each item neatly on the countertop.

"What are you making?" I asked her.

"I don't know. Something Khmer."

I didn't have to ask her anything else. I knew she was clueless. When my mother was younger, she knew how to cook many Cambodian dishes, but after I was born she stopped cooking them. Now she was good at preparing lasagnas and salads, things Grandma didn't care for. As Mom stood watching the vegetables and soy sauce and fish sauce, I knew she'd reached a dead end.

"Your friends already brought food over. Why don't we just serve that?"

It took her a while to answer me, and when she did she seemed all tired out. "It's your grandma's funeral. And she only likes Khmer food."

I left my mother and went to my room, where I could still feel my grandmother. I could smell her perfume, and the *prang khyal* she rubbed on her chest when it felt tight, and the incense she burned when she prayed and meditated; I could even hear the Buddhist chants that had become part of my breathing. Some sounds you can't ever forget.

I looked at my grandmother's bed, at the cream-colored comforter she liked so much, and I could see her in it. How all the parts of her face tightened when she slept. How her body remained in one position throughout the night, as if sleep itself was a task to endure. I pulled back her comforter and smelled the freshness of her sheets.

Then I tiptoed to the window and opened it. Mom had instructed Grandma and me to keep it shut and locked, but sometimes we would crack it open to let the night breeze in. Often we knelt down side by side in front of it. But there was no breeze that night. Everything was silent and lifeless.

One day when I was twelve, Mom and I came home to a flooded bathroom. Several years earlier, when I started school, Grandma had begun working at a factory, putting labels on clothes. That day she had left work early because she wasn't feeling well. She had wanted to shower before we got home so that she could have Mom *kaus khyal* her and then go to bed. We found her on her knees in the bathroom, mopping the floor with a towel and wringing the excess water into the bathtub. Water continued to flow from the sink faucet, and Grandma had placed a plastic container in the sink to catch it. When it got full, she dumped it in the bathtub.

I stood before the mess on the floor, unsure how bad the situation was. There didn't seem to be that much water, yet my grandmother couldn't control it. Mom dropped her tote bag and got down on her knees in front of the sink cabinet. She reached her arm far inside, and her face tightened as if she were in pain. Then, like magic, the water stopped.

"Why didn't you turn off the knob under the sink?" Mom asked.

Grandma's hair and the front of her shirt were wet. "Because I didn't know. You think I would let the water run if I knew?" She didn't sound angry at Mom, but at herself.

I believed that my grandmother would have been smarter if she'd learned English, but I was still shocked to discover that all of this mess could have been prevented if she had just known about the knob under the sink. Mom hadn't read any instructions in English on how to stop the water flow. She just knew, so why didn't Grandma? I watched them: one was so powerful, the other only a shadow.

That evening, Grandma lay in her bed with a tight chest and achy back muscles. As I got older, she became more and more fragile, almost like rice paper. Mom massaged her arms and legs as I sat on my bed with elbows on my knees and chin in my hands. Lately she'd been short of breath, and her feet sometimes swelled. The last time Mom took her to see a doctor, he prescribed diuretic pills to reduce the swelling. He also wanted her to return for all sorts of stress tests, but she refused to see him again. And my mother couldn't say anything to change her mind.

"Grace, go get the *prang khyal* and the lighter," Mom ordered.

When I returned with the tiger balm and lighter, my mother had pulled back Grandma's comforter, and Grandma had taken off her nightgown and was lying on her stomach.

Mom lit the candles on either side of the Buddha figurine on the altar and the sticks of incense in a jar of uncooked rice, and turned off the bedroom lights. Although it was still early, I felt sleepy. I sat on my bed and watched my mother caress my grandmother's skin. She took off the lid to the *prang khyal,* dipped her forefinger in it, and rubbed the clear tiger balm down the middle of Grandma's back. Then she picked up the half-dollar coin sitting next to the stereo and ran it down the area where she had smudged the balm. She ran it down the same spot over and over until it turned pink and then red. Grandma grimaced with pain, but she didn't let Mom stop. She said this ancient healing method made her feel better than the medicines doctors prescribed.

For as long as I could remember, we had used the same coin; its rim was now as smooth as the edge of a spoon. Mom *kaus khyal*-ed me once, and I clearly recall feeling as though the coin were tearing into my flesh. So I thought my grandmother was crazy. I would rather go to a doctor than get those welts any day.

About half an hour later, when Grandma's back looked like the red skeleton of a fish, Mom cleaned off the coin with a corner of the bedsheet. "Tomorrow you'll feel better," she said, and got off the bed.

I knew she was going to her room, where she would draw up math lessons and unit plans for the next two months. "Don't go," I begged.

"I have papers to grade," she said.

Grandma looked over at the door. "When I die, Chandra, take me back to Cambodia, or even to St. Pete—"

"*Mak*—"

"Daughter, take me back to a place where the people knew me. Where someone could say they remembered me. Don't leave me here, where I'll be lost forever."

"*Chas,*" Mom said reluctantly.

Grandma wasn't satisfied. "Give me a real funeral. Not like an American's. I have no one to depend on but you."

Without another word Mom blew out the candles and left.

When Grandma and I were under our covers, I asked if she felt better. "Don't worry," she said. But I did worry. I had already learned that dying was when you leave and never come back. And considering that there were only three of us in the house, we couldn't afford to lose anyone. But beyond the fear of losing my grandmother, I think I was more afraid of losing my mother. I was sure that without Grandma, Mom would be even farther from my grasp.

And without her, or my father, I wondered who in this world would claim me.

"Grandma's old?" she asked.

I shook my head, even though I knew she couldn't see me in the dark. "Old is okay."

"When you get old, you die without knowing about it first."

"That's good. Then you don't hurt."

"Grandchild is smart. But then you die before saying everything that you want to say."

I sat up in bed. "You can say everything now, Grandma. You can tell me about everything." My heart pounded in my chest and up into my throat as I waited for her stories.

But all she did say was "Go to sleep."

At the funeral home, the director, Mike Grubbs, was waiting for us in the lobby. When Mom had come in three days earlier to make the arrangements for the service, she had told him that there would be no more than twenty people attending. So now he led us down a hall with red carpet to his smallest room, where twenty folding chairs were set up in two rows on either side of the aisle.

On the opposite wall, in front of a beige room divider, stood a podium and a microphone. And in front of them was my grandmother, in a closed casket. I had begged Mom not to have a viewing of her body, and to my surprise, she didn't object. At the head of the casket was a wreath of white carnations. It hung at an angle, as if to shed light. Like the casket, it was strange and ugly.

I stayed where I was as Mom weaved through the chairs, sliding her fingers along them.

Mr. Jasper arrived promptly at one o'clock. He was an old neighbor who all the kids liked because he cussed and chewed tobacco. "So, so sorry, Chandra." He said her name like all the Americans did, pronouncing the "ch" as in *Charlotte* and not as a "j" the way Grandma had.

Mr. Jasper glanced over at the casket and started coming toward me. I politely waved to him and left to find the bathroom. I went into a stall and stood there, counting the minutes till the day would be over.

When I returned to the room for the funeral, Mr. Grubbs was talking to my mother. "We should start. It's one-thirty," he said to her.

I looked out at the space. Besides Mom and me, there were only twelve other people who came to show Grandma respect. Stacie, Rob, and Tracy, my closest friends from school, and Tracy's mom. Mr. Jasper. The young couple who had recently moved to our street with their five-year-old. Three of Mom's school friends. And an older woman whom I'd never met; my mother later told me she was one of Grandma's coworkers. They were scattered throughout the room like checkers on a board.

"Yes, we should start now. Whenever you're ready," Mom said to him.

Mr. Grubbs furrowed his eyebrows.

I was queasy. The guests were all watching, and I knew they were curious about what was happening.

"You have someone to do the service, right?" he asked.

Mom quickly glanced at me, and in that glance I began

to see her differently. No, she did not have anyone to do the service, although she knew she should. It was part of the arrangement she and Mr. Grubbs had made earlier in the week. But who could Mom have gotten to preside over the funeral? Certainly not a priest or minister. ·Grandma was a Buddhist! What could Mom do? She hoped. She hoped the way I did when I wasn't prepared for a book report and prayed that the next day would be a snow day and there'd be no school.

But because my mother had mastered the art of hiding things, she appeared unscathed by Mr. Grubbs's question, and it didn't take long for her to assure him that even though there were only the two of us, she and I, and neither of us looked official enough to conduct the funeral, we had everything under control.

"It's okay. We're Cambodians," I told him.

Mr. Grubbs sighed. "Well, of course."

My mother gently put both hands on my shoulders, pressing down on them. I reached up and placed my hands on hers. It was the first contact we'd had since Grandma's passing. My mother was not affectionate, so it would have been unfair of me to expect her to change all of a sudden, just because my grandmother had died. But the softness of her warm skin reminded me of hot porridge on a snowy day.

I found a seat in the front row that was reserved for the family. As I sat down, the five-year-old popped his gum. "Jimmy, be good," his mother warned him. I winced at the disrespect, content that Grandma's casket was shut and that she wouldn't have to see or hear the little runt.

Mom stood at the podium for exactly thirty seconds. "My daughter and I thank you for coming. We are touched by your thoughtfulness. My mother would have been grateful. Now, please, let's meet back at our house, where a light lunch is waiting for us," she said, smiling personally at each of us, and stepped away from the mike.

No one stirred as she walked away, but I felt their uncertainty. Had they heard her right? Was the funeral over already? Surely they hadn't showered and dressed in their most appropriate funeral clothes for this? But it didn't matter how uncertain they were. My mother was already waiting for them at the door.

Back at our house, while Mom worked on the food, our guests sat admiring the portrait on the wall. Mom came out and gave each of us a name tag. We held the white paper with a blue border, not sure what to do with it.

"Just in case you forget each other's name," she explained.

It was beyond peculiar to be wearing name tags at a funeral, but I didn't want to bring it to my mother's attention. I took my name tag with the large black letters and slapped it on my new black shirt, and everyone else followed. We looked up from our names and grinned awkwardly at each other. Jimmy's parents were now Bob and Tif. Mrs. Whitman was Suzanne, and the other two teachers were Jackie and Eleanor. And I already knew Tracy and her mom, Christina, well. Mr. Jasper, Rob, Stacie, and Grandma's one friend couldn't make the lunch.

"I hope you're hungry," Mom said as she handed out

plastic plates and utensils wrapped in white napkins. We filed into the kitchen. Mom had put a checkered tablecloth on our kitchen table, along with a vase of mixed flowers from Sparky's Grocery. She'd laid out a couple of casserole dishes people had brought us, plus her own baked chicken, Italian bread, corn, pasta salad, and a spinach salad. When I had opened the refrigerator that morning, I had seen the newly prepared dishes and known that there would be no Khmer food at Grandma's funeral, but I hadn't brought that up to Mom.

Back in the front room, with plates on our laps, Eleanor pointed to the painting on the wall. She was a tenth-grade teacher, and I had overhead Jacob, the love of my life, and his friends say that she was easy. "Not just with giving out grades, either," Jacob had said to his buddies. I would have her for English the following year.

"Chandra, that is a lovely portrait you have. That must be how old now—nine or ten years, right?" Eleanor asked. The others looked up from their food and agreed.

"Yes, Grace was only five then," my mother said.

Eleanor shook her head in friendly envy. "You haven't changed a bit," she told Mom.

"Neither did your grandmother," Tif said. "Good genes must run in the family. You're lucky, Grace." She pointed her fork at me. "All Asians are lucky. You can't tell how old they are. They all look young. And it's so sad your grandmother died so young."

There was a freeze in time as everyone broke away from their food and again remembered why they were at our house. The teachers put their half-eaten lunch on the coffee table and held their drinks close to their stomachs. Even Jimmy stopped chewing his bread.

It was Christina who started the conversation going again. "This is great chicken. Mine always turns out dry." Everyone agreed that the food was delicious.

"Well, Chandra, it must bring you some sort of comfort to know that you were there when your mother, you know, had her heart attack and died," Tif said. Her husband handed her his drink, which she pushed away. "Seriously, when my mom died. No one. Was there. She lost her balance getting out of bed when Dad was at work and all of us kids were at school. It was a freak accident. When we found her, her legs were all twisted. Sad. Dad never got over it." Her head seesawed until Suzanne confirmed that it was indeed sad. "So, consider yourself fortunate, you and your daughter. At least you'll find comfort."

"Yes," Mom said. "We are lucky. It was in her sleep, and Grace was there." Everyone, including Jimmy, looked at me. There I was, fully dressed for my grandmother's funeral, and yet I'd never felt more naked.

"Oh. That must have been upsetting for you," Tif said.

I heard every single word Tif had said, and as I looked out at all of them—including Mom, who had not asked or said anything to me about the morning Grandma died—I knew they wanted something from me. But I didn't know what to say. I didn't even know if I was obligated to say it. All of these people who hadn't known my grandmother well enough to even remember that in person she looked different from the picture wanted to know about her last night. Were they entitled to the gross details of her life when they didn't even know her name?

I turned to Mom. It had been a long day, and I knew all she wanted was to rest so she could return to her life and teach her students again. She could sleep well tonight if I said that Grandma hadn't made a single sound in her sleep. That she had left this world without a single bruise to her body or heart. But I wasn't sure; I knew only what I saw that morning. *I'll tell you,* I said to my mother in my mind, *I'll tell you but not them. I'll tell you that when I woke up I found Grandma with the comforter tangled around her legs, and she was not breathing, but her eyes were opened. I'll tell you that I knew right away, that I didn't even bother to shake her awake. That I went down on my knees and cried into her soft scarred belly, crying like I'd never done before, crying not because I thought I would miss her but because I needed her.* "Please," I said to her, "please help me to be full."

I looked around at everyone in our living room. "No, I'm okay," I said.

One by one, our guests began to pick at their food again, smiling gingerly at my mother and me, telling us how lucky we were to at least have each other. And at that moment, I knew that these people saw us the way I saw us in the photograph: incomplete.

3

Mom was in her room working on tests when Grandma asked me, "Did you know your mom was a dancer once?" She and I were in the basement folding laundry. I was eleven, and I shook my head, wondering why she would think I would know that important piece of knowledge about my family. How often had either of them shared anything about their past? Grandma put down the blue towel with the white flowers. "I'll show you."

I stood against the dryer, feeling the heat warm my back as she walked to a box in the corner. It was the size of our microwave, and it was tied up with a white nylon rope. I'd always been curious about that box, but I was never allowed to see the contents.

Grandma cut the rope with scissors, and the white pieces fell onto the floor. She reached into the box and brought up whatever she had been looking for. She handed me a thin, flimsy photo album. "There were many young dancers, but your mom was everyone's favorite. When she was on stage, she smiled so brightly."

Grandma proudly opened to the first picture. It was of Mom, about thirteen years old, standing at the center of a stage. Her fingers were long and curved back. Behind her was a heavy-hanging black curtain, on which colorful Cambodian letters were pinned. She was dressed in a ruby-and-gold-colored bodice, with a swath of the same material draped diagonally across her chest and over one shoulder, exposing the other. Her skirt was tea length, and folded in multiple pleats down the front. Gold bangles wrapped around her arms and ankles, and a glittery, high headpiece set off her long black hair. Four other similarly dressed girls were spread in a semicircle behind her, and all of them held small gold bowls in their right hands, their left legs raised up behind them.

I pointed to the bowls. "What are those for?"

"It's the blessing dance. It's to give good wishes to the people. Inside of those cups are rose petals. See?" Grandma showed me the next picture, which was of the dancers reaching into their cups. The next one was of red petals scattered like confetti at the edge of the stage.

When we finally came to a picture of Mom and Grandma together, my heart plunged deep down into my stomach. In the picture, Grandma was kneeling before Mom, securing the dance bangles around her ankles, and Mom was facing down, with her hands on Grandma's shoulders for support. I lost my breath. There it was, one of the things I'd always wanted, a piece of their past, and I was holding it in my hands.

"Your mom was crying here," Grandma said as she pointed to my mother.

I studied the photo more closely for traces of tears but couldn't find any. Until my grandmother's death, I'd never seen my mother cry. When I couldn't find any tears in the photo, I realized that my grandmother's mind was clouding up again. "No, Grandma. You're wrong. Look. You see, you were helping her with her dress. For the dance. Mom wasn't crying."

My grandmother shook her head. "Your mom was so upset. She was crying."

"No, she wasn't." I pointed to the bangles and the skirt and the headpiece.

Grandma threw the album on the floor. "I no stupid! Why no believe?" she hollered in English.

I picked up the album, believing her now, deciding that only an honest person could be that outraged. I trusted that passion and truth belonged together. But then what awful thing had taken place to make my mother break into tears? "Okay, Grandma," I said softly. "Okay. Then why was she crying?"

My grandmother pulled away. "Why your mom was crying?"

"Yes. You said she was crying. Why was she crying?"

She pointed again to her daughter in the photo. "Oh! Your mom was crying because her friend's brother was getting married, and your mom couldn't be a bridesmaid like the other little pretty girls."

"Really? That's it?" Of course I would have cried, too, if all of my friends were asked to be bridesmaids and I wasn't. But there had to be more to what my grandmother was telling me. "So what happened then?"

"Nothing happened."

Trying to get any information from her or my mother was like a scavenger hunt. "Nothing else happened? What made her stop crying?"

"I told your mom that I would hit her if she didn't stop crying. I told her she should be ashamed of herself."

Without another word from her or me, my grandmother took the album and buried it deeply in the box. She took the roll of white rope from a drawer and began to wrap it around the box. Then she knotted it, and knotted it again, seeming satisfied.

At baggage claim in Florida we had no one to greet us. No grandparents who hadn't seen us in ages, or aunts and uncles to pinch my cheeks, no friends to welcome Mom back home. Not even cousins to check me out. Tracy had said that when she saw her girl cousins in New Jersey, the first thing they did was compare breast sizes. I was already a B cup, so I was sure I would have a good chance of winning. But it was just my mother and me. Me with my Abercrombie backpack hanging off one shoulder and Grandma in my hands, and Mom scouting for our one small suitcase. She had told me to pack light since we would be returning in two days.

As I scanned the airport, I saw an Asian woman wearing

a pair of gold hoop earrings the size of bracelets. But she was different from the Asian women who walked their kids to school in Pittsburgh, and definitely different from the ones who bought twenty-five-pound sacks of rice like us. She wore white jeans, carried a brown Louis Vuitton purse, and the top half of her hair was pulled back in a red scrunchie, which I wanted desperately to tell her was out of style. At first I caught her in the corners of my eyes, and then I had to look at her as if I was looking at myself in the mirror. She had dark skin, but other than that she looked nothing like me or the woman I would become someday. Yet there was something that we shared.

"Grace," Mom snapped, "stop acting like you've never seen a Cambodian before." I quickly turned from the lady to Mom, then back to the lady, before it sank in: there were more of us.

The first thing Mom said when she got behind the wheel of our white Dodge Neon was "It's so hot I can't breathe. For heaven's sake, who can live here and not go insane?"

We got on the Franklin Bridge, which was the longest bridge I'd ever been on. The cars zoomed past us as if we were in a race, and I held on to Grandma even more tightly than I had on the airplane.

I hadn't expected there to be so many cars or buildings, or so much water. It was blue, a perfect reflection of the heaven from which we had just descended, and it stretched far, so far out that I couldn't help thinking that the chance of the bridge snapping in two and us falling into the water was better than the chance of a boy reciprocating my affection.

"This, Grace, is the Tampa Bay. What do you think?"

"It's beautiful."

"I hate it. Always hated it."

I left Mom alone, and tried to scan past the water—looking out at everything she and my grandmother had left behind. And out, too, at all the things that my father had witnessed. Which tree, which light pole, which mark in the road had he seen that I was seeing now?

Mom was right: it was hot in St. Pete. The car was air-conditioned, yet I could almost see the heat living outside. Even the plants and grass seemed to have a hard time breathing in the thick air. As we got off the bridge, the thin, tall palm trees with their fingerlike leaves emerged.

The roads were smooth and wide. No potholes for the tires to dip into and make our jaws snap. We began to glide forward with the rest of the traffic. Mom switched lanes and cruised between two SUVs. When we got off at an exit that led into a busy district, my mother pointed to the businesses she remembered: the mall with an indoor skating rink, the old Chi-Chi's building she went to for her senior class banquet, and other companies that she didn't say anything about but just named: Dick's Bicycle Shop, State Farm, a dog salon. I wanted to ask about the songs she had skated to or the friends she had had dinner with, but I kept my mouth shut, afraid that my questions would only silence her.

We turned the corner at the mall, and she pointed to a

hotel with a red roof: La Florida. "I guess we can stay there," she said. "Hopefully, there will be a room."

The first thing I did when we entered our hotel room was place Grandma on the dresser, right in front of the mirror.

Cramped from carrying her around all day, I shook my arms and spun around. "It's still early. Let's go do something. Let's go see where you used to live," I said.

"What?" Mom took a step back from me. "Why?"

"Why? Mom, we're finally here. Don't you want to go back to where you grew up? And see the people you grew up with? The people Grandma knew? You know, don't you have friends you want to hook up with?" I gave her a wink, wink.

"No. If I wanted all of that, I would have come back a long time ago. We came here for a funeral."

"Yeah, but—"

"Grace."

My stomach churned at the sound of my name coming from her mouth. It was the sound of getting into trouble for speaking in class without first raising your hand, or the "you should know better because your mom's a teacher" sigh. It was full of exhaustion and disappointment.

It was unfair to be in school 24/7. But it didn't matter how I felt. "Yes?" I said quietly.

She went to her purse and pulled out a twenty. "Go to the mall."

The mall was only two blocks down from the hotel. For a late Friday afternoon, the food court was quiet.

There were a lot of old people, though: ladies with curly white hair, dressed in pinks and greens, some the shade of celery and cucumber, their husbands with eyeglass cases in their pockets. I ordered a small frozen yogurt at Baskin-Robbins and claimed an empty table in front of the arcade.

I took out my scrapbook, which had started out as a journal in the sixth grade. On the first three pages, I had written about the school's cheerleading captain, who—I was fairly certain—was crushing on our school principal; my mother; and Jacob, who was three years older than me and didn't know that I was planning on marrying him someday. I turned the page to my dad's picture, tracing his face a couple of times like I always did.

I knew that Mom would be furious with me for what I was about to do. But I had no choice. I had to bring the photo of him to Grandma's funeral. Someone, I was certain, would be able to recognize my father and tell me where to find him. And I would just have to deal with my mother's wrath later.

I heard a couple of girls laughing and carefully closed the cover of my scrapbook. There were three of them, all with long straight hair parted in the center and dyed light brown. The smallest one, whose waist was almost as thin as my ankle, needed a touch-up; her black roots were showing. The loudest one was chunky with a square-shaped behind. Her lips were outlined with some sort of red pencil, but the lips themselves were bare. I couldn't really understand what they were talking about because she was laughing too loudly.

After much concentration I finally made out what the third girl was saying. "That dude was *chkourt.*"

I didn't know what *chkourt* meant and pretended to look at my scrapbook again as I continued to eavesdrop on them.

"*Aneung chkourt,* for real," the thin girl said. And they laughed again.

The chunky girl added, "He's so crazy, man." And I finally understood that *chkourt* meant "crazy"! Her voice was deep and sexy, but more than that, it brought to me a realization. They were combining Cambodian and English, and the new concept that Camglish existed made me so delirious I finished the rest of my yogurt in one bite.

When they laughed again, I joined them, and at first I didn't realize what I was doing. But when I did, I gave it all I had. I brought forth all the laughs from the pit of my stomach and let them out, looking right at the girls to show that yes, I completely understood their Camglish. *Oh, yes, I'm one of you,* I was saying. The chunky one finally noticed me and . . . what did I do? . . . I winked. At the snap of my eyelid, she shut her mouth and hit the other two girls in their ribs. And all I could think was *Did I really do that? Did I really wink at her?* Without waiting for the answer, I winked again, and then again, in the other eye. And I couldn't stop winking. My lashes were out of control. I quickly looked down and rubbed my eyes, pretending to have problems with my contacts, until my vision blurred.

After several minutes I looked up from my scrapbook, and they were gone.

※ ※ ※

Mom had left me a note on the pillow: *Will be back soon.* I crumpled it and threw it across the room, where it bounced off Grandma and onto the floor.

I took off my shoes for the first time that day, and the air from the AC seeping in between my toes felt like a cool morning in October. I drew back the curtains and saw that the sun had turned orange and the clouds around it had darkened. The noise from the traffic wasn't as loud as it had been earlier, and it was quiet now in the pool area, with only a handful of people lounging around. I was thinking of taking a walk there and just dipping my feet in the water when I saw my mother. She was in a lounge chair with her hair in a ponytail. A few loose strands swept into her eyes, but she seemed unbothered. She had a book on her lap and was holding an ice cream bar in her right hand, half eaten. She looked so relaxed and serene. And I wanted to scream, because I didn't think any of this was possible for her, to have hair in her eyes, to slowly nurse an ice cream bar. With Grandma and me, she'd always been busy, busy, busy. What else was there about her that I hadn't thought possible?

4

It had only been last April, the Spring Fling. I was walking down the stairs in my purple strapless dress when I saw Grandma sitting at one end of the couch. Mom was waiting for me at the door, the keys dangling from her hand. We would need to pick up Austin, Randy, and Tracy. Randy was my "date," and Austin was Tracy's. Randy wasn't a true date because my mother wouldn't let me go out alone with a guy until I turned sixteen.

"Don't go, Grandchild," Grandma said. Mom never agreed with me, but I always thought that my grandmother's burn reddened whenever she was overwhelmed with emotion. That day her left cheek took on the color of a pomegranate.

All week she had pleaded with Mom to keep me home, but I didn't understand why. I knew that she worried about me catching colds or scraping my knees or even a boy touching me in the wrong places, so hearing her begging me to stay sent a sour taste down my throat. But all week I'd planned for this night, finding the nail polish to go with my dress, flipping through magazines for hairstyles. As much as I wanted to relieve my grandmother of her worries, I couldn't pass up this dance. A couple of my friends had told me that Randy was going to kiss me.

From the couch Grandma said to Mom, "She is too young to dress up for a boy."

"A lot of teachers will be there. I will be there," Mom said.

"Things can happen. I don't want her to regret anything later."

And that was when I realized that my grandmother's not wanting me to go to the dance had nothing to do with me and everything to do with my mother. "Regret" had often visited our home.

If we hadn't been about to leave the house, Mom would have asked what "regret" it was that Grandma was referring to. Grandma would not really answer, though. But they both knew what the regret was.

In the car Mom rolled down her window, and we drove to Tracy's house in silence.

My grandmother was old-fashioned. She sometimes fidgeted when a love scene came on TV. My mother was not. Still, strangely enough, I had never seen her with a man. Everyone knew that the seventh-grade science teacher had the hots for her. Once he even asked me about her after class. I thought that a date would put her in a better mood, so I told her about him. "He's a good teacher, and he's fair," I said. Mom wasn't interested. She had never been interested.

A long time ago, I had decided that she couldn't get over my dad. She and he, unmarried, had made wild, passionate love, but for whatever reason, they couldn't stay together. But what was the reason? Had my dad not wanted to marry her? Was that why she and Grandma took me away from St. Pete, so that Mom wouldn't have to see him again? But why wouldn't my dad have wanted to marry her? Had he been too immature? In his defense, he had only been eighteen years old. Surely Mom would have known that guys mature at a slower rate than girls. If given the chance, he would have grown into the perfect husband and dad, and then Grandma wouldn't have made Mom feel so ashamed for not having a husband. And there would be no "regret."

After Mom returned from the pool, we drove to Flannegin's. The young and perky hostess wore a tiny purple apron around her waist and took a pen from its pocket to write down our name. "It's a forty-five-minute wait," she said apologetically. It was a Friday night, and the restaurant was crowded and loud. TVs hung from the ceiling in the bar area, and framed pictures of celebrities and the skyline and coast of what seemed to be St. Petersburg decked the walls. A fish tacked to a wooden board on a pole sang "Don't Worry, Be Happy" whenever someone walked by, which was too often.

By the time our waiter showed us to our table, I was so hungry I felt nauseous. I didn't wait for him to take my drink order or list the special for the night. "Chicken fajitas, please," I said. "With guacamole. And water."

After he wrote down my order and left, Mom said curtly, "You should wait and be more patient next time."

"Why? I already know what I want—I'm starving."

"Grace, there are proper ways of doing things." She was trying to keep her teacher's voice in check so the people at the next table wouldn't look over.

Our waiter returned with two glasses of water and took Mom's order. A chicken salad with house dressing on the side.

"You can have some of my food when it comes," I offered.

She politely shook her head, and silence fell. Apparently, she had nothing else to say to me.

I, however, had a lot I wanted to say that night. Like that I thought she was so beautiful, and that even though my friends often complimented me on my own features, I was still hoping to look just like her someday. Or that I liked to watch her play with her earlobes. Or that I liked the way men gazed at her when she walked into a bank or store, and that I hoped I could one day achieve the same thing—with the boys at my school. But I didn't say any of that.

I could hear the TVs from the bar and a kid pounding his fists on a table not too far from us, but it was so quiet in the space that Grandma's death had created for Mom and me. It was like a box that she and I were held captive in. My grandmother wasn't there to start conversations about the nice lady at work who brought her boiled peanuts for lunch or how the price of a whole chicken went up and up. "When will it stop?" She was not there to ask Mom what was good to eat at the restaurant, or to open her menu and pretend she could read the words for quesadillas, clam chowder, or dessert. She was also not there to argue with Mom—which, I was learning, wasn't as comforting as I had thought it would be.

"Sooo. I'm excited to be in high school," I said.

"Good," Mom said, and sipped her lemon water.

"Four more years, then off to college I go." I gave her an outrageous thumbs-up.

"That's right, four more years."

We went back to politely nodding.

I snapped my fingers. "I already know what I'm going to major in."

"Grace . . ." Her tone made my stomach churn again. Why was she disappointed now? "Stop trying to grow up so fast. You're just a kid."

"I'm not that much of a kid. I'm four—"

"Grace, do you know what I did when I was fourteen?" she asked, tilting her head.

"What did you do?"

"I wrote checks to pay the bills. I called the water delivery people to set pick-up and drop-off dates. I called your grandma's doctor to see what the holdup was with her blood work."

This—Mom's list of chores when she was a little girl—was never a topic of disagreement between her and Grandma. Grandma sometimes said that Mom had been the perfect daughter. And whenever she complimented

47

Mom, I saw that her soft, normal cheek turned slightly pink and her eyes got a little wet. The compliment, of course, only made life tougher for me: it wasn't easy to be in a league of perfection.

"Well," I said, "I can help you with some things. I mean, I could write checks for you."

"Please. You're being stupid now," Mom said.

Both of us turned quiet. Of all the middle school teachers, my mother had the most accelerated students in her classes. She would come home with stories of how so-and-so would accomplish this or accomplish that later on in life. "I won't be surprised if someday we see Mecallah in an astronaut uniform on CNN." Or, "That Josh will be too smart for his college professor." I didn't dislike hearing stories about Mecallah or Josh or Mom's other gifted students. I had to admit that those kids were striving for great things. I was just not one of them. But I also knew that I wasn't stupid.

I did everything I could to hold back my tears. *I am fourteen, I am fourteen,* I repeated to myself. *I will not cry, I will not cry. Just because she called me stupid doesn't mean that I am. I will not cry.* And I didn't, not technically, anyway. My eyes were just a little wet, and they stung.

"I didn't mean it that way," Mom said. "I mean, Grace, why would you want to take on more responsibilities than you have to? All I'm saying is that you're a kid, enjoy the moment." I rearranged my fork and spoon, and she groaned. "Stop crying. Why are you so sensitive?"

"I'm not crying, I'm not sensitive, and I'm not stupid," I said quietly. "I was just trying to help."

Mom took in a deep breath, and let it out. She did this three times. "I know you're not stupid. You . . . you always think I'm the bad person. I'm not. And you always ask so many questions. I'm just trying to protect you, to let you be a kid."

"Protect me? From what?"

She put up her hand as though it were a white flag, and didn't notice our waiter standing nearby with our food. I looked away so he wouldn't see my wet eyes.

"It's hot," he said, and placed the sizzling skillet in front of me.

I waited for him to walk away before I took a soft tortilla and spread guacamole down the center. "I just wanted to tell you that I know what I want to be when I grow up. I thought you would be proud of me."

"You already know what you want to do?" She sounded genuinely perplexed and pleased.

"Yeah. I've always known it."

"Well, what is it? And please, don't say a movie star or something absurd like that." She subtly pulled back her shoulders and playfully raised them up and down as though she were a teenage pop star. This was why kids at school were crazy about her. As much as they feared her sternness, they loved how she would unexpectedly break out into a joke during a lesson or sing with them while walking down the hall. I did, too. I just wished she did more of the joking and singing at home, with me.

"I want to be a teacher, like you."

"Really?" She returned to her lettuce, twirling a long lemony-green piece with her fork, like it was spaghetti.

"Yeah, really. Why are you so astonished?"

My mother stuck her fork in one of the tomato wedges and began to laugh. I asked her what was so funny. "It's crazy being a teacher. One day you love your students, and the next day you thank God they're not yours."

I bit the inside of my cheeks. "Did you use to think that about me? When I was in your classroom? I mean, wish that I wasn't yours?"

"What?"

"If you were pregnant before you left St. Pete, why didn't Dad try to talk you into staying?"

She put on her serious teacher face. "He didn't know, not when we left."

"Did anyone know?"

Mom picked up her water, thinking of what to say, I was sure. "We didn't tell anyone."

"Is that why you didn't bring me here sooner? You would be embarrassed when people saw me?"

She sat up straight. "No. It had nothing to do with you."

I wasn't sure if I was comforted by my mother's answer. I was glad to know that I wasn't the cause of her not bringing Grandma back to St. Pete, but at the same time I selfishly wanted to be in the center of her world.

I fixed her a fajita, and we spent the next few minutes eating. Once, I had accused her of loving her students more than me. "You hate me. I bet you regret having me," I had said. I had meant what I said, and I had expected her to be angry, and in the heat of it to profess her love for me. Instead she had walked out of the room and had given me the silent treatment for a week. Later Grandma had told me that I had hurt Mom's feelings. *I . . . hurt . . . Mom? Was that possible?*

"Your mother buys you clothes. She feeds you, and you say she doesn't love you? No gratitude," Grandma had said to me.

I watched Mom finish the fajita. "So, what about my dad?" She looked up at me, confused. "When he found out, did he wish that I wasn't his? Is that why you guys didn't get married?"

Mom leaned in closer to me. "Grace, I met your father when I was very young. On my prom night."

"I know that already. But was he cute that night? Was he all decked out?"

She ran her finger around the rim of her glass, which squeaked.

"What is he like?" I asked, looking around the restaurant for him, believing in miracles. "What are his favorite songs? Does he like country music? Or . . . or does he listen to Dahlia in the evening, like you? What does he smell like?"

Mom gave me an "I can't believe it" look. "I don't know. That was so long ago."

"What about my dad's family? Are they here in St. Pete, too?"

"Grace, how many times must I tell you that I don't know?"

"But how do you not know?"

She picked up her fork and raked the bottom of her plate with it.

"Grandma's gone. You and he are the only two people I have. And you're still trying to hide things. Why—"

"Grace. Stop."

I waved my double-jointed pinkies at her. All six of my other fingers were normal; my crooked pinkies, however, I used to gross out my friends at lunchtime. "Look at these. Did I get these from him?" I popped my pinkies out of joint over and over.

She placed both hands on the table. "Stop it."

I looked away.

"Darn it," she said under her breath. "I can't wait until all this is over."

The waiter came by with our bill, and Mom thanked him. Then she said to me, "Grace, if that lady over there came here and asked you where you're from, what would you say?"

I turned to see an old woman with gray curly hair stirring her iced tea. She put down her spoon and grinned at me. "I don't know. Pennsylvania?"

Mom smiled tiredly at me, and I knew that my answer was wrong. I had forgotten that what I was supposed to say was "Cambodia." "You are Cambodian. You are Khmer, Grandchild," Grandma would remind me. "Don't forget that. You do not have yellow hair and white skin like *Americ*. We are different. We are from Cambodia."

"If people were to ask me, I would say 'Cambodia,' " Mom said.

"Well, yeah, you were born in Cambodia."

"But I've lived here for most of my life. I am a U.S. citizen."

"Okay, then you're American."

"No, on paper I'm American. Once you're a Cambodian, you'll always be a Cambodian."

"Okay. What's wrong with that?"

Mom's eyes wandered around the restaurant again, like they were searching for something she could hold on to, for something to save her. "There's nothing wrong with that. But for some people, the beliefs that they and their community grew up with—whether they've been proven to be right or wrong—are so much in their blood that those beliefs begin to tell them what to do. And that's when it's wrong. Doing things and saying things just because that's what has been done and said."

"What did my dad do that was wrong?" I asked.

My mother opened her mouth, and I heard a faint sound coming from it when she closed it. Her shoulders relaxed. "I'm not hiding anything from you. I just don't want to talk about it. There's a difference. Hopefully, when you're older you'll understand."

Like her, I hoped that I would understand, but not about the difference between hiding something and not wanting to talk about that something. I wanted to understand her. My grandmother. My father. Me. I wanted to understand me.

Mom grabbed her purse and got out of the booth, and I followed.

Mom woke me up the next morning in the hotel room. "Come on, we can't be late," she said. She had already showered and was ironing her dress, with a towel wrapped around her body. I was groggy, and scratched my head a couple of times before I could sit up, tasting the foul onion from last night's dinner. Mom had drawn back the curtains, and the early sun was hot on my face. "Go shower."

On the road, my mother was nervous that we would not make it for the service. But at the speed we were driving, we couldn't possibly miss Grandma's Cambodian funeral. Mom quickly pulled into the Albertsons parking lot, where there were only a couple of cars. Inside the store she told me to stop strolling around—there wasn't time for that.

After she paid for bags of apples, oranges, bananas, and two honeydews at Albertsons, we went to Tran's Oriental Store. Standing at the door was the cashier, a short lady with pudgy cheeks and a pout, and who was in desperate need of a makeover. The first thing I would offer her was a tube of lipstick with moisturizer. She neither smiled nor greeted us. *I am here for my grandmother's funeral and I can still manage a grin, so what's wrong with you?* I thought. Mom went to the back of the store and picked up red candles and a long box of incense sticks, and then she returned to the front for a couple of *num ansarm* tightly wrapped in banana leaves and bound in thread.

As we loaded all the bags in the trunk, I asked Mom what the food was for. "For *sain,*" she quickly answered, and got back inside the car. "Offerings to Buddha and Grandma, so that she doesn't go hungry."

"So, what's going to happen at temple?"

She turned at a light. "What do you mean?"

"It's a Saturday. People go to church on Sunday. So who will be there today? What will they do? What will we do?"

She drove around a neighborhood of small ranch houses, some with gardens of white and purple periwinkles. "There will always be someone at temple for service. And you have the monks. They do chants, like the ones you hear on Grandma's tape. They eat. We eat. And we leave."

"That's it?"

"Yes, why?"

"We came all the way here just for that?" I hadn't meant for it to come out as an accusation.

Mom looked at me crossly. "Well, she wanted a Cambodian funeral, and I'm giving it to her. What more do you want?"

"Aren't Grandma's friends coming, at least?" I was thinking that I needed people at the service to see my dad's picture.

Mom stopped at a corner that we'd already turned at three times. "Where is it?" she muttered to herself. But she didn't answer my question, and I realized that Grandma's Cambodian funeral would be another lonely service like the one we had had for her in Scottsville.

Mom reached over and ran her hand across the nameplate on Grandma's urn. "Make sure it's stuck on tight. I don't want it to fall off after we leave."

"What? Aren't we going to bring her back with us?"

She braked at a red light and glared at me. "No, Grace.

She stays here. That's why we brought her here. This is where she wants to be. I'm trying to do this last thing for her, okay?"

My throat closed up, and I held Grandma tightly on my lap.

"Oh, don't cry now," Mom ordered. "This is supposed to be a good day. I'm trying to do a good thing, and I don't want you to ruin it!"

I looked out the window. "I'm not crying. I just don't want to leave her here, that's all. We have to bring her back."

"Grace, I can't deal with this now."

I held on to my grandmother more tightly, seeing her and me sitting at our bedroom window. I couldn't believe it would be so easy for Mom to part from her mother. Had it been this easy with my dad?

"There's the temple," she said with relief, and pulled up to a small house that was painted orange and yellow.

She gasped.

A For Sale sign with a Sold sticker was posted on the front lawn.

5

It was our first Fourth of July celebration. It would also be our last. I was seven, and I had waited all day to go to the lake for the fireworks. July Fourth brought out wild lawn ornaments in Scottsville. Balloon flags. Red, white, and blue streamers trimming trees and bushes. Some older men strolled down the sidewalk or into Quick Mart in their colonial uniforms, as if they were on a movie set. And flags were raised at almost every house.

I was the first to wake up, and I folded my towel and took out the sunscreen bottle from under the sink and placed them in my favorite bag. In the afternoon, while Mom graded papers I helped Grandma pack for our picnic. Hot rice in tinfoil. Beef jerky that she'd dehydrated two weeks earlier. Pickled carrots and cabbage. Bananas steamed in sweet rice. And watermelon. She promised that there would be enough for me to share with my friends.

Now that I'm older, I can look back at that day and appreciate the few hours at the lake that my grandmother spent laughing with her mouth open. Or when my friend Tracy came over to our picnic area and my grandmother brushed our hair and tied it with tinfoil. For the rest of the afternoon, Tracy and I skipped around the lake, blinding people in the process.

But later that night, I could only remember my grandmother with a towel wrapped around her head. Right before darkness set in, after we'd eaten most of the food and walked Tracy back to her parents, when mosquitoes bit our legs and the bugs started a chorus, when families huddled close together for what we'd been waiting for all day, my grandmother asked Mom to take us home.

"No!" I said.

Mom wrapped an arm around Grandma and said, "You'll be okay."

Grandma listened, and as the gray of the evening turned into night, she stood quietly next to Mom. But with the first *pop!* of the fireworks exploding, she yanked our beach towel off the ground and tied it around her head and rocked. It was a sight of misery. Suddenly aware of how crazy she must look to other people, I felt eyes on her, on us. We were the fireworks they were watching. Grandma wasn't ill like the old man down the street who needed a nurse to bathe and feed him, or the mentally challenged kid who attended school for two hours each day just so he could be around kids his age. But she would do something like that, wear a large towel at a fireworks celebration as though she had a head wound.

Purple and silver lights burst in the sky when Grandma cried to Mom to take her out of the jungle. Without further consideration, Mom gathered my grandmother into her arms, and although I didn't want to, I quickly packed our belongings in Mom's "Teachers Are the Best" tote bag. When we reached the car, my mother said to Grandma, "We are safe and out of the jungle."

I threw the bag into the backseat and yelled, "There's no jungle. It's a park. A freakin' park!"

After Mom put Grandma in bed at home and pulled her blanket up to her chest, she sat me down in the living room. Each time she wanted to teach me a lesson, she'd wear her strict teacher face and speak to me as if I were her student. I hated her tone, but I wanted so much of her to be in me. She held her back straight and folded her hands in her lap. "Family is not embarrassment," she finally said, enunciating each word as if it were part of a new vocabulary. When she asked if I understood, I nodded.

And I did understand. Unlike Mom and me, Grandma knew only a little English. When she wanted the price of a vase or rug, she asked the salesperson, "How much this?" Instead of taking me to Burger King, she took me to Hamburger King. And if a person wasn't married, then the man or woman was *"sing girl."* Most of the time she called me *"Grrreh."* I wanted my grandmother to go to school to learn English so that she didn't ask what was happening on television when my friends were around or where to sign her name on a form. But Grandma was the woman who held me when Mom was unhappy that I hadn't put the lid back on the rice pot or when I had failed to clean my hair off the bathroom counter. And for that I was grateful.

What I didn't understand was her and Mom. Almost anything, from the brand of a fish sauce to a hairstyle an actress was wearing on the red carpet to even how many incense sticks to burn, could amount to a disagreement and then an argument between the two of them. But no matter how they felt about each other, no one else was allowed to feel that way. Once when Grandma asked a theater usher where the bathroom was, he shook his head, and instead of asking her to repeat herself he took the easy way out and looked at Mom, expecting her to translate. My mother stood before the usher and squinted, waiting for him to redirect his question. When he didn't, she said, "What, are you not hearing well today? My mother wants to know where your restroom is. That's right, your *restroooom*. How hard was that?"

That night, after Mom finished lecturing me, I went to bed and lay awake, certain of many things. With my father around, not only would there be more happiness in our small family, but things would be easier. Grandma would never wear a beach towel around her head. Mom would see me as her daughter, not just as a student. And I wouldn't have to try to understand my mother and grandmother.

Mom got out of the car and walked to the door of the "sold" temple and knocked on it. When no one answered, she put her ear to it. Then she looked through each window.

I followed her, and when I could, I got on my toes and peered in, too. The rooms were empty.

While Mom canvassed the backyard, I walked over to what used to be a garden. There were remnants of tomato plants; a couple of small red fruits had fallen and were drying up in the soil. At one end I saw a patch of tall lemongrass. When the light breeze hit us, the blades rustled against each other, making a sound like a faint wind chime. I broke off a blade and smelled Grandma standing over the stove cooking a Khmer dish. It was the pungent fragrance of garlic, tamarind, and fish sauce all mixed together.

Mom found me. "Well, they're not here. No one's here. The place was really sold," she said resignedly, with her hands on her hips. "Can you believe it?"

The sign up front was a dead giveaway, I thought. "I'm sure we can still find the temple that they moved to."

"I don't even know where to look." It was one of the few times she sounded helpless.

"Phone book. The Internet. We can go to a library."

"This was not meant to be."

"It is," I said, thinking about my father.

She went to the steps leading up to the back porch and sat down. Drops of perspiration had collected on her forehead and were rolling down the sides of her face. "What was I supposed to do?"

I shrugged.

She gave a half laugh, the kind that shoots out of your nose. "I bet you're right, Grace." I shrugged again, having no idea what she was talking about. "I bet I was supposed to gather up all of her friends, everyone we used to know, and do a big funeral for her, to send her off happily to nirvana or heaven, or wherever her next life is. And you know what, I wish I could. Just so I wouldn't have to worry about her anymore." She sighed. I had a feeling that she was waiting for me to say something, and when I didn't she continued. "How was I supposed to do that, Grace? We've been gone for fifteen years. Did she think I could just call everyone up and invite them to her funeral? They didn't even know where we were. That's her, Grace, she always wanted things her way without thinking how it might affect other people. Like no one's opinions or feelings mattered. Like no one else mattered. Darn it—I give up!" She stood up, swung her arms into the air, and then looked down, her shoulders slouched.

I felt sorry for my mother, but I was also puzzled. Wasn't she the one who "always wanted things her way"?

As we left the backyard, a young thin Asian man walked up. He had a clean face with bright eyes, and was probably in his late teens or early twenties. At the sight of Mom his lips slowly widened in at first an unsure and then a full grin. For a brief moment, I was perturbed that he didn't notice me the same way. I was my mother's daughter—I must have had some of her looks!

"*Bang* Chandra!" he exclaimed, calling my mother big sister. After hearing how he pronounced Mom's name, I knew he was Cambodian. And I was no longer angry, but ecstatic that Cambodian men could be this hot.

"Chet?" my mother finally asked, bewildered. He

moved in to hug her, and after a couple of seconds she put her arms around him.

Chet pulled back and finally saw me. I was glad that I had opted for the black wedges and not the flat sandals when we left Scottsville.

"Chet, this is my daughter, Grace. Grace, this is *Bang* Chet," Mom said.

He shook my hand. "Hey."

I gave him my biggest smile. "Hi, *Bang* Chet." Big Brother Chet.

"So, *Bang* Chandra," Chet said, "how is your mom?"

"She died. Two weeks ago," I said.

"Oh," he said sadly. "She was nice. Really nice." After dutiful seconds of silence, he updated us on the temple. "The community finally raised enough money for a new building. It's almost complete. They just sold this place. I'm here to pick up some of the tools we forgot in the garage, and I'll be on my way back." His voice got higher, like a schoolboy's. "You and Grace should come with me. Nahrin is there with a lot of people painting, and I am sure he'd like to see you."

I clapped my hands but stopped in midair when Chet and Mom turned to me. She told him that we didn't have time, that we had to pack for our return flight.

"Mom," I said, "the plane doesn't leave until tomorrow afternoon. It's perfect now. We can take Grandma to the new temple for a visit, and we can bring her back home with us tomorrow. We can probably give her a funeral service, too. Right, *Bang* Chet?"

He shook his head. "The new temple isn't ready. The monks are in Alabama right now. And we're trying to finish the temple as fast as we can so that they have a place to stay. There's a big wedding next weekend." He paused. "And I think the monks would need time to plan for a service."

Mom jingled the keys in her hand and stepped toward our car.

"Everyone will be so happy to see you," Chet said to her.

"We have to go."

Chet put out his arm. "It's okay. Just wait. I'll be right back." And he ran to the back of the temple.

When Chet returned from the garage with his bag of tools, he told Mom to follow him, and gave us his cell number in case we got separated. "Later we can go back to my house. My mom will kill me if you don't come by." He ran to his car, and before he got in he said, "She talks about you and your mom all the time."

My mother looked at me, dumbfounded.

"We should go," I said, trying to hold back my urge to do a cartwheel. "We can't offend him now."

We followed Chet in his black Acura. Mom scooted down in her seat and put her sunglasses back on. She turned on the radio and played with the switches until she came to Mix 100.7. Then she started tapping on the steering wheel when the commercial for Albertsons came on. *Albertsons. Crazy about food.*

"Did you like shopping there?" I asked.

"Not really. There was one close to the house, though." Her voice tapered off, and I wondered if there was more she wanted to say. From the corners of my eyes, I saw her feathering out her hair, something my friends and I only did when we had someone to impress. Chet couldn't possibly be this someone, though, because he was way too young for her. And I refused to think that she was a cradle robber.

"What?" she asked.

"Who's Chet?"

"A member of a family your grandma and I knew." A respectable answer indeed, but one that didn't tell me much.

"And who's Nahrin?"

"His older brother." She faintly smiled to herself again, and I wondered about this Nahrin who was making her blush.

Mom pulled off the main road onto a dirt path. It led us to a large, new building with a brown roof. A couple of cars and trucks were parked along the path, and she found a spot behind Chet's car.

When she got out and started talking to him, I ran my hand through my hair and mentally assessed how I looked. Black wedges, black capris, and a white knit top. Casual yet stylish. A mature young lady.

"Come on," Mom said.

Chet flashed me only a quick grin before the two of them started walking, with me following behind. Clearly, he had yet to appreciate my sophistication.

"All of this land belongs to the church," Chet said excitedly. "So we can build additions in the future."

Although the property was big, up close the temple was not so large, only the size of a drugstore. Most of the walls were white and still chalky, and the grass around them needed to be trimmed. In the front lawn there was a hole the size of a wading pool, all ready for a pond with lily pads, lotus, and koi.

I approached the sculptures standing on pillars at the entrance of the temple and touched their delicate-looking stone fingers.

"They're statues of Apsaras—traditional Cambodian dancers," Chet said. "Your mom used to be a dancer. My brother has pictures."

Mom looked away uncomfortably.

Several men and women were planting flowers and bushes, preparing the walls for painting, and building chests. I studied each face as carefully as I could, but none of them resembled my father in the picture.

The less good-looking men were shirtless, revealing hairy chests and beer bellies. The more stylish ones like Chet were sporting crisp white tees and cargo shorts; I didn't know how they planned to paint looking like this. The women were wearing pants and long-sleeved shirts.

"They're afraid of turning dark," Chet whispered to me. I studied my own skin—brown as a roasted peanut. Had I known that I was to strive for light skin, I wouldn't have lain out in the sun so much.

I heard the men and women speaking Cambodian, although I couldn't clearly make out what they were saying.

The sound of it was loud, exciting, friendly, and carefree. The easiness of it was what bound all of these people together, I realized. Maybe this was why Grandma hadn't cared to learn perfect English.

"Are these all the Cambodians in St. Pete?" I asked Chet.

"Of course not. There's a large community here."

"Well, of course not," I said—trying to play it cool. "I knew that."

"Wait here," Chet said to Mom and me.

Cambodian music played in the background, and each time the woman's falsetto voice got crazy high, I had to cringe. When a new, upbeat song started, I tapped my foot to the rhythm and snapped my fingers, and a couple of people glanced over at Mom and me. "Act properly," she whispered. I didn't know what she meant until she sharply kicked my foot.

I didn't think Mom, who was standing stiffly, knew any of the people. We awkwardly smiled at them, and I gave a couple of the men and women a big wave with a "Hi. How are you?" One older man nodded halfway at me, and I heard him say in Cambodian to his friends, "American kid." I realized he didn't approve of me when a couple of them chuckled. Under her breath, Mom ordered me to drop the hand, and I immediately dropped it like I was a robot. She then placed her palms together, right below her chin, bowed slightly, and said, *Chumreap suor.* The people returned the same greeting. I followed her gesture, and the same people chuckled again. But this time they dropped their paint rollers, shovels, and hammers, and came to us.

They smiled as they asked where we were from, where the rest of the family was, and why we were here. As Mom was about to explain the reason for our visit, Chet returned. And he brought Nahrin with him.

I could see immediately why just the thought of him would make Mom run her hand through her hair. Nahrin was shorter than his brother, but stockier and more muscular. He had high cheekbones, a rectangular nose, and when he saw Mom his smile stretched wide, revealing perfect teeth. His arms were massive; as I looked at the veins rivering down his forearm to the back of his hands, I thought sadly about the black-and-white photo I had of my father.

At first Mom didn't look back at Nahrin. I could see that she wanted to focus on anything—the buttons down his linen shirt, the yellow and orange paint cans behind him, and even his open-toed Tevas—so she didn't have to focus on his face. When she finally glanced up at him, I lost my breath. There was something that they were reading in each other's eyes that I was not familiar with, except what I had seen on movie and television screens. The look was forceful, hungry, shy, and longing. Chet and I were still standing nearby, but it was as though we were invisible. And the only thought that came to my mind was, *Was he before or after my father?*

One man asked Nahrin if he had known Mom for a long time.

Nahrin cleared his throat. "Yes. I knew her and her family before she moved away."

Silence followed, and a few minutes passed before the

busy men and women left us. I watched them walk away in a group. One man slapped the back of another and told him to come over for dinner later. They would grill steaks, the kind with a lot of fat.

Nahrin moved his hand forward, but stopped short of touching Mom. "Wow," he said, sliding his hands into his pockets. "You haven't changed much."

"You haven't, either," my mother said faintly, pulling me to her side.

Chet pointed at me. "She's *Bang* Chandra's daughter."

I waited for Mom to tell Nahrin my name, but her mind was apparently full of something else. Nahrin didn't seem surprised to see me, but he didn't say anything, either. So I said, "Hi, I'm Grace." He gave me one of those light polite touches on the shoulder, like he felt sorry for me. I didn't know exactly what I was expecting from him, but that wasn't it.

"Chandra, I'll show you around," Nahrin said. When he said her name, his voice was warm and milky, delicious to hear.

Mom rubbed my shoulder, and I was shocked to feel her touch. But before I could ask if she was all right, she told Nahrin that we had to leave.

He looked confused.

I looked at him, his younger brother, the people working around us, and the almost-finished temple, and the weight of my fervor to stay in St. Pete until I found my father was so strong that I thought I would fall from it. "Our plane doesn't take off for another day," I said, and Nahrin turned to me gratefully.

69

"Great! I'll show you the garden." He took Mom's elbow and pushed her toward the back of the temple. Chet and I shrugged and followed them.

The land was expansive. When I asked if the tall old pine trees in the back were the temple's, Chet said yes, that 3.6 acres belonged to them. As we continued across the land, Chet kept his distance from me. His hands were in his pockets, and his eyes wandered. I realized that I didn't have much to offer him, but the fact that he thought I was too childish for him was beginning to rub me the wrong way. I knew I was too young for him, but where was the polite small talk?

"How old are you?" I asked him when Mom and Nahrin were in the garden.

"What?"

"How old are you? You know, age-wise?"

"Twenty. Why?"

So he was a twenty-year-old who thought he was all mature and wise, like Anderson Cooper. Not a chance. It didn't take me long to think of something that might make Chet sweat. "Just wondering. You seem much younger than that. That's all."

Chet opened his mouth to say something, but changed his mind.

"What?" I snapped.

"Nothing."

"You wanted to say something, so say it." I had lost any air of sophistication, but it was worth it. I was on a mission, and I didn't have much time for small talk anyway.

"How old are you?" he asked.

I saw the numbers in my head. They were small, baby ones that had no years to them. Beginners that had so much to learn. "Almost fifteen." I didn't wait for his response. I straightened my back and focused on Nahrin and Mom. The wind had swept her light, carefree laughter over to us.

"Fourteen? *Bang* Chandra left here about fourteen years ago."

"I know," I said quickly.

Chet's eyes were tiny and quizzical. His mind was running, and my heart beat faster. It hadn't occurred to me until then that Chet might know my father. "She and my grandmother moved right after Mom got pregnant with me. Do you know my dad? I never met him." As soon as I said it, I regretted it. I had made Mom out to be easy like Eleanor the English teacher, when in fact she was the most prudish thirty-three-year-old woman alive.

Chet looked stunned. "Sorry, kid."

My cheeks felt hot, and it wasn't because I hadn't gotten the answer I wanted. It was because of the sympathy that Chet wore on his face. "Well, of course you didn't know," I said. "Jeez. I just meant . . ." As I tried to come up with an explanation, Chet walked closer to me.

He put his arm around me. "It's okay."

I moved in closer so that his arm covered me as much as possible, and smelled the scorching sun on his T-shirt.

When we got to the garden, there were no vegetables, not even baby ones. It was a large plot of rich soil that stank of manure. I later learned that Nahrin had an MBA, and he worked for an insurance company. But in the evenings and on weekends, he volunteered by keeping track of the temple's finances. He thought they had enough property to turn a quarter of it into a minifarm where they could grow exotic fruits to sell at the flea market. They were starting off with mangoes, and eventually they would go into longans and persimmons.

"Do you know what longans are?" Nahrin asked me.

"Well, yeah. Aren't they white fruits in a sweet, thick syrup? We eat them all the time. Grandma used to buy cans and cans of them," I proudly answered.

He tsked-tsked. "Oh, no. If you've only eaten them from a can, then you've never eaten real longans. Real, fresh longans are fleshy, sweet, and tender."

"The ones in a can are, too," I said, as though I was giving a book report.

"Sure. But the ones in cans don't let you really appreciate the fruit. Fresh longans practically melt on your tongue. You have to bite into the shells and peel them off. It takes work to get to the meat of the fruit, but when you do you see how perfect and beautiful it is. And when you eat one, you can't stop. Now, are longans from the can the same way?"

I looked from Mom to Chet, and then to Nahrin, who had the biggest grin I had ever seen. And I looked at Mom again, who was also smiling. I didn't know what had changed in the last thirty minutes. "Well, I don't know."

The three of them started to laugh. Nahrin rubbed my head, like he'd known me all of my life. Like I was so endearing that they couldn't help but make me the center of their universe. And even though I refused to wear anything from the kid's department and I had my own line of Clean & Clear to use at home, I really did want to be endearing that day, especially to my mother, who was laughing like I'd never heard her laugh before. But I still didn't find what I had said funny.

The dark pit of my throat balled up, and no matter how hard I tried or how much I hated it, I couldn't hold back any longer. But even as the tears trickled down my cheeks, Mom's and the two brothers' cheery, distorted faces told me that they hadn't picked up on my feelings.

I ran to Nahrin and wailed into his chest, "I don't know what you're trying to say!"

And, finally, when I let go of Nahrin and stepped back, they were staring at me, astonished.

6

We were inside an office with a large wooden desk, a black leather chair, and two other chairs with maroon cushions, glass walls surrounding us. A crystal globe sat on the desk, and the banker handed it to me. I was six years old, and, standing at the corner of his desk, I rolled the globe over and over.

Mom and Grandma sat in the cushioned chairs, Grandma dressed in her fancy black pants and a white shirt with a lace collar. Mom wore shorts and a pretty green shirt. It was Saturday, and she had said that I could run errands with her after we dropped Grandma at home.

I looked at the clock on the wall, and I concentrated on counting the minutes. We'd been in the office for twenty minutes, but it felt like twenty hours.

Five brochures were laid out on the banker's desk for

my grandmother to see. I ran my hand across them. "Which one do you want, Grandma?" I asked.

Mom shushed me. The banker smiled.

Grandma pointed to a green brochure with a picture of a family standing in front of a house. "What is this one?" she asked Mom.

"Money market," Mom answered.

I could have told Grandma the same thing. The banker had already explained it.

Grandma pointed to the smiling banker. "Ask him again what it is."

"Why?" I asked, and then in Cambodian, "He already told you." I would have not traded my grandmother for anyone else's, but at that age I would have changed many things about her. For one, her lack of English. I was sure as I could be that if she knew English, then Mom and I wouldn't have to sit there with her in the bank. I would be in Mom's car, and we would be driving from shop to shop.

No one seemed to have heard me that day in the bank. Or if they did, they didn't care. Looking back, I saw myself as the typical whiny, impatient kid. But when you're six and all you've been waiting for all week is your mother's attention, you fight for it.

"Can you explain this again?" Mom asked the banker.

After he did, I listened to Mom translating how much money Grandma would need to put in the bank and how much interest she would get. I looked at the clock again; only five minutes had passed.

Grandma pointed to the next brochure.

"This one you can't really take money out until you retire," Mom said.

"Ask him again," Grandma insisted.

I decided that my grandmother could use my help. "You should study English. I'll teach you." She pretended to not hear me. Mom pulled my arm, and I went to stand beside her instead.

After we'd been in the bank for one hour and twelve minutes, the banker asked if we had any more questions. Mom asked Grandma. Finally, my grandmother shook her head.

"Okay, which plan do you want?" Mom said.

Grandma giggled, and I wondered what was so funny. "I don't know which one," she said to Mom. "You pick."

We pulled into Chet and Nahrin's driveway, and Mom said that she hoped I wouldn't have another breakdown. I wasn't sure how to take her comment—but I liked to think that she was concerned about me. The day was clear and so sunny that it looked almost a little yellow. As I focused on the houses lining the street, my eyes stung. The flat, long houses were painted flamingo pink and lime green, some with big white garage doors. Palm trees were scattered around the yards, and bushes were neatly trimmed under the windows. A balding Asian man down the small street was mowing his lawn.

We headed toward the front door, and a grinning, tall, plump woman came out and sauntered to us. Her salt-and-pepper hair was pulled tightly back, her pudgy face free of wrinkles. She waved to the lawn-mowing man, her arm flapping up and down, before she saw her younger son and called out his name, "Chet . . . Chet." Then she saw my mother.

"For real, *Mak*, it's *Bang* Chandra," Chet happily confirmed in Cambodian.

Mom placed her purse on the ground and *chumreap suor*-ed the woman. The woman flung her arms around Mom and squeezed her. When my mother was out of the tight hug, she asked in Cambodian, "How are you, *Oum*?"

"I'm okay, *Coan*," the woman answered, calling my mother "child." Then she looked at me. I handed Grandma to Mom, forwent my American wave, and *chumreap suor*-ed her also. She didn't give me a chance to introduce myself before she hugged me, too. Her meaty arms were cool and soft, and her full breasts under my head were like my grandmother's pillows.

When she let me go, I said slowly in English, "I am Graaace."

"I am *Oum* Pall-aaa," she replied equally slowly; apparently, she didn't have problems with English.

Inside the house, Nahrin strolled to the sunroom and turned on their wide-screen TV, and Chet retreated to another room. Mom followed *Oum* Palla into the kitchen with the grocery bags from our morning of shopping. I didn't know where to go, so I hung around the dining table, fingering the long oak table. A beige sateen tablecloth covered it, and an arrangement of blue and pink silk flowers sat on a lazy Susan.

I walked to the living room, where a long black leather sofa took up one wall, rounded the corner, and took up another wall, facing the entertainment center that housed silver bowls and artwork from Cambodia. On the top shelf was an altar; a picture of Buddha in a black frame rested in the back, and in front of him were candles, incense sticks, and fresh fruits, all on silver plates or in silver cups. I sat on the sofa and placed Grandma in the center of their glass-top coffee table.

Mom and *Oum* Palla walked in with plates of the fruits that Mom had bought. *Oum* Palla's eyes were teary and red, and she blew into a tissue. Mom put the plates of oranges and apples on the altar, and *Oum* Palla began to light sticks of incense. She handed three of them to Mom and another three to me, before lighting three more for herself. Then, carefully, she picked up Grandma and placed her on the altar, where, I assumed, she would be visible and revered by those who walked by. *Oum* Palla pushed the coffee table in toward the cavity of the sofa so fast that I had to climb over one arm of the sofa to get out. She and Mom sat on the floor, with legs folded to the side, and I joined them.

Immediately, *Oum* Palla began a chant that lasted only a few seconds but was followed by many, many minutes of silence.

I can't usually be pensive when I am forced. Even in school, during the moment of silence, I don't know what I'm supposed to think about. The soldiers who died for this free land? The men in white curly wigs who wrote the Constitution? Or bad cafeteria food? But that day in *Oum* Palla's living room, I thought about my father, wondering if he could feel my presence in St. Pete.

Finally, *Oum* Palla stretched her legs and stood up.

Mom and I did the same. I reached up to bring Grandma down. "Don't, *Coan*," *Oum* Palla said. No one had ever called me "child" in Cambodian, and even though it was coming from a stranger's mouth, the sound of it was much more comforting than my own name.

"Why?" I asked.

"Leave her there," she said, which wasn't a real answer. I looked at Mom for an explanation, but she only nodded.

They walked away, and I followed.

"Chet, Nahrin, set the table," their mother ordered.

The guys poured glasses of water as Mom and I carried out dishes of stir-fries to the table. Before we sat, *Oum* Palla brought plates of dried fish and pickled watermelon slices.

"Should we wait for your husband?" I asked.

"We would be waiting for a long time," she said.

Chet whispered that his father had died seven years ago.

"Sorry," I said, even though I knew how useless the word was.

Oum Palla sat at the head of the table, and her sons took the two chairs across from Mom and me. We waited as Nahrin scooped each of us a plate of hot rice.

"How was the temple?" *Oum* Palla asked her sons as we began to eat.

"Great," Chet answered.

"What about the roof? Did those men come back out to fix the loose tiles?" She had directed the question at her older son, who was pretending not to hear her. "Are you listening?" Her words were short, but the tone, a pleasant wail, softened the meaning.

"Nothing's wrong with the roof," Nahrin said. "Besides, *Mak,* it's brand new, so we have a warranty."

Oum Palla frowned at him. "Well, you better do things right the first time so that you don't waste energy fixing them the second time. If anything goes wrong with that building, *Yeay* Mao is going to beat you until you faint."

"Who is Mao?" I asked.

"*Yeay* Mao is very old, so you call her *Yeay* or she'll be angry."

What? She was the first person I knew who wanted to be called Grandma.

Oum Palla nodded at Nahrin. "She does not want anything to mess up her daughter's wedding. Don't say I didn't warn you."

"Mom, please don't yell at me now. We have important guests with us today." Nahrin raised his left eyebrow at Mom flirtatiously.

Oum Palla rolled her eyes at him. And Mom blushed as she pretended to concentrate on her rice.

"Chandra, do you remember Maly?" *Oum* Palla asked. Mom glanced up from her plate, and her voice trembled when she answered that she did. "Well, she's the one getting married. Her fiancé, David, is from a different state."

"That's wonderful," Mom said.

"He lives in Seattle," Chet added. "Oh, by the way, how's Atlanta?"

"We live in Scottsville," I said. "In Pennsylvania."

"Is that where you've been living all of this time, Chandra?" Nahrin asked.

Mom nodded.

"What about Georgia? Didn't you go to college in Atlanta?" *Oum* Palla asked.

Mom put down her fork. "It didn't work out in Georgia." Then she coughed a fake cough. "There are so many new people here. I didn't know anyone at temple today."

Oum Palla agreed. "Are there a lot of Cambodians in Scottsville?"

"No," I said, jumping in. "We're the only ones."

"Oh God." *Oum* Palla sat back in her chair, dismayed. "Not a single Cambodian?"

"We are the only three." I showed her my three middle fingers. Then I dropped one of the fingers.

Oum Palla looked thoughtfully at me. "We have a lot of Cambodians here. In this neighborhood alone we have about five families. *Yeay* Mao doesn't live too far from us. And in fact, one other family lives on this road." She hit the table with her index finger to show how close that family was to us. "They moved here just a year ago."

We continued eating until *Oum* Palla rested her elbow on the table and held her chin in her palm. "Why would Naree want to live somewhere with no Cambodians?" I hadn't heard my grandmother's name in so long that it sounded almost foreign when she said it. Naree. I thought it was pretty enough to be the name of a flower. "Why?"

"Yeah," Chet chimed in. Then he said to Mom, "You left so suddenly."

"How do you know?" *Oum* Palla asked in Cambodian. "You were still a kid with his nose running."

"I remember," he answered, looking at Nahrin.

Oum Palla told her son that he talked too much. "How do you expect to find a wife if you talk more than she does?"

"I have a girlfriend, so I'll have a wife eventually."

"Who? That American? You're going to marry an American?"

I was amazed that she would find the idea so hard to believe. Could that be why Grandma hadn't wanted me to go to the Spring Fling, because she was afraid I would end up marrying an American someday?

"What did you expect, *Mak*?" Nahrin teased. "He's an American, too."

Chet bit into a piece of the salty fish and sucked on a sliver of the sour watermelon, saying nothing. But I knew what he was feeling—that it was hard when someone tried to tell you who you were.

Nahrin gazed at Mom. "Are you going to move back home, Chandra?"

"Oh, my job is in Scottsville. And Grace's school is there. It'll be too hard for her if we move now." She jabbed her fork into the rice. As we watched the top of her head, I thought I was the only one who knew that she was not hungry for food.

Nahrin's eyes remained on her, hopeless now. "Then why did you come? I mean, after so many years. Why did you choose to come now?"

When Mom didn't reply, Chet spoke. "*Bang* Chandra wants to give *Oum* Naree a Cambodian funeral."

Nahrin took a deep swallow, and I could see the tip of his Adam's apple moving up and down. "That's all? You only came for your mother? I should have known." The disgust in his voice made Mom stop eating. She quietly laid down her fork and spoon and stared at her half-filled plate.

Oum Palla told everyone to stop the interrogation. "This is not *Judge Judy.*" When the table turned quiet, she said that Mom could take Grandma to temple next Sunday, after the hustle and bustle of the wedding. "Of course, the funeral is very important and should be given first priority, but *Yeay* Mao will kill anyone who tries to interrupt her daughter's wedding."

"We're going back tomorrow," I said.

"What?" she asked with her mouth full of food. "When did you get here?"

"Yesterday, and we're going back home tomorrow."

"You were planning to stay only three days. How did you expect to give a funeral in only three days?"

I didn't know what to say, and Mom didn't answer.

"That is not okay," *Oum* Palla said in Cambodian. "Chandra?" Mom looked up at her. "You need help doing this. Of course you do. You don't know all the requirements for a funeral. Stay until next week so that we can do it properly for your mother."

Stay for a whole week? Could this be possible? I found Chet nodding at me, as though he knew what I was thinking and hoping for.

"I can't—"

Nahrin cut her off. "She can't, Mom. She has to go back to her life in Scottsville."

"Chandra?" *Oum* Palla said.

"*Chas*," Mom answered.

"It's up to you. I'll let the monks know to prepare for a funeral service. And I have a phone directory of all the Cambodians here in St. Pete. Every family is listed. It's in there, in the drawer. I can call everyone for you. But you do what you think is best for you. Do you want to give your mom a Cambodian funeral or not?"

"She does," I said. "She thinks my grandmother will be hungry and lost if we don't."

No one heard me.

"I want to." There was a crack in Mom's voice. "I want to do everything right for her."

"Then call your work and tell them that you have to take a week off to take care of your mother. If this is what you really want, do it now so that you don't regret it later. There really is a point in time when it's too late."

"*Chas*," Mom obediently said.

Had I heard my mother correctly? I quickly turned to this new woman sitting beside me, wondering what happened to the one who had given out instructions and orders. Wasn't she worried about her students and lesson plans and tests to give?

"We stayed in a hotel last night," I said to *Oum* Palla. I waited for Mom to kick me under the table, but she didn't. Instead she filled her spoon with white morsels and lifted it to her mouth.

"We have room here. We're like family here, you know." She'd said the word "family" so casually, and even though I couldn't comprehend the extent of what that F-word meant to her, I couldn't help but get the sense that

84

I was where I was supposed to be. And that feeling would make anyone feel almost at home.

"Yep," Chet said. "Your grandma was family enough that she spanked me and Nahrin a couple of times."

"Your skin is so thick it probably didn't even hurt," Nahrin said.

To me *Oum* Palla said, "You and your mom can have the extra room. After lunch, Nahrin, take Chandra to the hotel so that she can bring her things over."

I woke to a *whack, whack, whack.* I was sleeping in the spare bedroom, which was at one end of the house, across from *Oum* Palla's room. Soon after Mom called to change our flight to next Sunday night, she and Nahrin took off to return the rental car and to pick up our luggage at La Florida. Chet drove out to see his girlfriend, and *Oum* Palla said it was her nap time.

The small extra room had a full-size bed pushed up against a corner, leaving only a niche for an old dresser and a narrow walkway to get around. On the wall above the bed was a large, open wooden fan dressed with plastic red roses and blue ribbons. "This is a special bed," *Oum* Palla had said when she showed us the room. She sat on it, the mattress swallowing her behind. "It was the first big item we bought when we came to America about twenty-five years ago. It was a happy day. We had saved money from recycling aluminum cans. Your grandma was there. She helped us load it up in the truck."

"My grandmother?" I asked.

"Yes, that's what I said."

After the nap, I found *Oum* Palla squatting on the kitchen floor with a butcher's block before her, a cleaver in her right hand, and a basket of fresh fish. To her side stood a high pile of fish heads and glistening black guts.

"You're up," she said warmly.

"When will everyone come back?"

"I don't know. They're grown people. Chandra and Nahrin will return once they get your things. And Chet, I'm sure he's still with his girlfriend."

"Oh, okay." I turned around to go back to the room.

"You don't want to stay here and talk with me?"

It was disconcerting to wake up in a different state, a different house, with no one around but an older woman I'd just met. Mom wasn't here to connect me to any of these things, or to *Oum* Palla. But I didn't want to be by myself. "Yeah. Sure."

I leaned against the refrigerator, and tried not to breathe in the stench. The kitchen was small and narrow, with one side occupied by appliances and the other by the sink and cabinets. A large rice cooker sat beside the microwave on the counter; the red Warm button was still lit. The pungent fish odor didn't permeate the house but hung in the open space of the kitchen.

"What are you doing?" I asked.

Oum Palla whacked off another fish head—the knife hitting the wooden block with a thud—and threw it onto the pile. The force of the blow had pulled her body forward and back in a single quick motion, as if she were a tree branch caught in the wind. Then she scraped off the scales; the white disks flew around her, some landing

86

on her arms and hair. "I'm cleaning fish. Haven't you seen this?"

I shook my head.

She cut open the belly of a silver mullet and scooped out the intestines. "How can you be a Cambodian daughter and not have seen anyone clean fish?" She smiled.

I didn't know how to answer her.

"One of Naree's favorite dishes was *trei khar,* and I'm going to cook a big pot of it for the funeral next weekend," she said.

I still didn't understand this business of cooking for the dead, but knowing that Grandma got to eat her favorite meals made me think that she wasn't too far away— maybe just a couple of hours' drive.

"You speak really good English. My grandmother could hardly say anything," I said.

"We led different lives." She ran the cleaver up and down the sides of the fish, and a couple of the scales, the size of my fingernails, fell into my lap.

"Where did you learn to do this?" I asked.

Oum Palla pointed to her fish. "This? I started doing this when I was five."

"Five!" I hadn't meant to be loud. She started laughing, but I didn't think it was that funny.

"Oh, yes. Things are very different in Cambodia. Especially back then."

What *Oum* Palla had said was not new to me, except that Grandma had spoken in Cambodian and started with "Grandchild . . ." Mom would usually interject that "America is different."

That was Mom's explanation for all their disagreements. But as many differences as *Oum* Palla, Grandma, and Mom thought lay between Cambodia and America, I thought there was only one. The language. It was a fogged-up mirror, a layer covering what was already there and preventing you from seeing what was really underneath.

"Oh, yes. Your grandma and I used to go fishing together all the time. We would take our baskets to the lake and scoop for catfish. Then we would bring them back home and clean them for our mothers to cook. No boys in the village could catch more fish than your grandma and me," *Oum* Palla said proudly.

"My grandma did that?"

"Yes. Why do you sound so surprised?"

"She never told me."

I watched her gut a new mullet, and a yellow tube fell out. A thin blackish cord attached the tube to the inside of the fish. She gently tugged on the cord to release the slimy tube of eggs and then placed it on a saucer.

"Your grandmother was an amazing woman. But some years in Cambodia were too hard. Not everyone can talk about them." *Oum* Palla got up and placed the cutting board and knife in the sink, the basket of fish on the counter, and the heads and intestines of the fish in a large plastic bowl.

As much as I didn't want her to stop talking, I could see that she was tired. Her back was the same as Mom's when she stood at the kitchen sink and pretended that no one was around. I got up, too, and made my way toward the spare bedroom.

"Do you know what I'm going to do with the remains?" *Oum* Palla asked. I quickly turned around. She held out the bowl to me. I shook my head, and she pointed to her backyard. "You see those trees?" There were several of them, but two, one with long, thin leaves and the other with shriveled brown berries, stood clear in my view. "They were this size when I got them." She stuck her pinky in front of my nose. "The secret to their growth isn't expensive fertilizer from Home Depot, but ugly, smelly garbage that no one wants anything to do with. I dig holes around the trees and bury fish heads and innards in them. I know from experience. Trash turns into sweet mangoes and longans. You understand?" she asked.

I told her that I did, that I got Bs in science.

7

Grandma shut her car door, and Mom started the engine. I was twelve, sitting in the backseat, and I could tell it would be a pleasant drive back home. Mom had just won the Innovative Teacher award, her second in her teaching career.

After the year-end awards ceremony it had taken us a while to get out of the school auditorium. Mom seemed concerned that Grandma would need to get to bed soon, but Grandma insisted that Mom stopped to talk with the students and their parents who swarmed her, wanting to congratulate her. I stood by my grandmother as Mom shook their hands and introduced us to the parents.

"He just raves about you at home," one mother said to Mom, and then to Grandma and me, "You must be so proud of her."

"Yes," I said.

To Grandma the mother went on about an assignment Mom had given her son. "She challenges him to think broader. Not giving him any crutches to fall on. Sometimes that's what you need. To jump off a cliff and not know if there is a net to catch you. You just need to do it. When you are put in that situation, you will fight. And when you fight for something, you will win. And if you don't, at least you tried. There needs to be more teachers like your daughter, don't you think?" the mother asked.

"Yes. Yes," Grandma answered, her head gently going up and down, her smile so wide. Usually when she spoke English, her "yes" could mean anything. Most of the time it meant that she agreed with you, even though she didn't understand you.

But that night, the pride on my grandmother's face told me that she had understood each word the lady said.

In the car, Grandma held Mom's plaque and said to her, "I want to take your award and show it to people at my work."

Mom laughed softly. "*Mak*, I'm not a little kid."

"Who cares? An award is an award."

As we pulled into our street, Grandma turned around to the backseat. "Grandchild, your mom always does things the best. Study and be smart like her. Don't be stupid like me," she instructed.

"*Chas*," I said.

Then she sucked in her lips, shaking her head. "If only she'd listened to me all the time. *Sday nas*." Regret.

※   ※   ※

Oum Palla got up from the dining table and answered the phone. It had rung many times that Saturday evening, and like Grandma, she answered each call, afraid that she would miss something important.

"Yes, yes, yes," she said loudly in Cambodian to her caller. "*Bang* Mao, give me your pants and I'll shorten them for you. But no, I can't sew your dress! Who said I can sew dresses? Why would I pay someone to sew my dresses if I know how to myself?" *Oum* Palla had a wide grin on her face, but she was still speaking as though she was hollering. "Okay, okay. I will come right over."

She quickly hung up the phone, and on her way to her bedroom she told Chet and me to get ready. We were going to visit *Bang* Mao.

"Who is *Bang* Mao?" I asked Chet. The three of us had been sitting at the dining table talking, waiting for Nahrin and my mother to get back from returning the rental and picking up our things at the hotel.

"Her daughter's the one getting married this weekend."

Oum Palla returned. "Hurry," she said. Chet aye-ayed her.

I followed *Oum* Palla to her bedroom and waited at the door. It was the master bedroom, with a full bathroom and a walk-in closet, both taking up one end of the room. She had her bed pushed into a corner, leaving a large space for her work area, which was marked off by a blue and red area rug. A factory-size sewing machine with spools of purple, black, brown, beige, yellow, and pink sitting atop it stood on the rug. She sewed for a company that let her bring work home. Two boxes of linen pants and shirts rested beside the machine.

Studying herself in the mirror on her dresser, *Oum* Palla unpinned her hair, let it dangle down her shoulder in one long coil, and then rewrapped it into a fresh bun at the back of her head, which she tacked down with bobby pins. She tugged at her T-shirt and then she raised her arms and sniffed at her armpits. She asked, "Do I smell like fish?"

"You took a shower, right?"

"Showers don't wash away death." She pulled out a new tee from her drawer, turned away from me, and changed her top. Her back was brown, with dark bumpy spots.

"What should I wear?" I asked. She scanned me up and down and said that I was fine.

I didn't want to be fine, though. Who wanted to be fine, when you could be drop-dead gorgeous?

Oum Palla hurriedly walked out of her room, the flats of her feet slapping the ground. I followed her through the house and into the garage. She opened the deep freezer and pulled out the bag of fish that she had just scaled. She squeezed the lumps in the plastic grocery bag to see how many fish were in there. "That grandma talks too much," she said in Cambodian. I thought she was referring to *Yeay* Mao. "You take too long to get ready, then she says that you're trying to impress men. Look at me." She stood up straight and pointed to herself. "Do I look like I need a man?"

I focused on the roundness of her belly and promptly answered, "No."

Oum Palla shut the freezer and walked back into her house. I followed her to the foyer, where Chet was waiting for us, and we both bent down to put on our shoes. "And if you don't take enough time, then she says you are sloppy. That grandma talks too much." From her tone of voice, I thought *Yeay* Mao was a very good friend of hers.

"Why do you care?" I asked.

She grimaced as she tried to push the heel of her foot into her pumps. "I don't care. The problem is that everyone else cares. You have one person who cares enough to repeat what she says, and then you have a whole problem to fix. That's why old people like me do everything we can to not let everyone talk."

"Who's everyone?"

"The community," she said impatiently in Cambodian. The actual translation, though, was "the town" or "the country," which were both comparable to the world. I looked at Chet and thought: *Wow, Yeay Mao is one freakin' powerful grandmother.*

It was not dark yet when we started walking. The air was warm, and from somewhere that I couldn't place, the sound of cicadas vibrated, keeping the evening in constant motion. Then, out of nowhere, a small lizard skittered at my feet, and I grabbed Chet's arm.

"What? No lizards in Scottsville?" he asked.

"No. We have cute animals there."

Chet bent down and picked up a four-inch lizard that was about to climb a tree, this one browner and bigger than the last, its tail wagging. The reptile was trying to jump out of his hand, but Chet kept it in his palm. A couple of times it yawned like it must have had a hard day of running around. "See? Isn't he cute?"

I didn't think so. "We have wild turkeys and deer." I loved deer, even when they ate Mom's hydrangeas.

"So, turkeys are cute to you?"

That was what pissed me off about people his age. They spoke to you as though they were the adult and you were a mere child. "Fine, turkeys aren't cute. But at least they don't kill other animals like that thing you're holding."

"Yeah, but that's what animals do. They kill to eat so that they can survive."

I rolled my eyes. "Yeah, I know."

"But you don't have to worry about this lizard." Chet laid it down, and it quickly crawled into a bush. "They eat mostly plants. Once in a while they'll fight each other, and one dies. And you'll see it on your sidewalk in the morning, all bloody, part of its stomach hanging out. And by the afternoon the ants will be swarming all over—"

"Stop," *Oum* Palla demanded.

"Yeah, stop," I echoed, amazed at how immature people his age could get.

At the end of the street, we took a left, and we walked along a wooded path through pine trees. The air began to smell like rotten eggs, and Chet said that it was the smell of sulfur from the water plant on the other side of the trees.

Oum Palla picked up her pace. I wanted to suggest to her that we should slow down, especially if she was concerned about her body odor, when she mentioned my grandmother. "*Yeay* Mao, your grandma, and I used to walk together all the time. Like this, side by side."

"Did my grandmother live in this neighborhood, too?"

"No. I'm not talking about here. I'm talking about Cambodia."

"Oh," I said.

"Naree and I came to the United States together. We lied on our paperwork that she was my sister, so that she could join us. Only immediate family members could come together. Otherwise, she and Chandra would have been stuck in the refugee camp in Thailand for a very long time. They didn't know anyone here to bring them over. My husband did, so that's how we got sponsored so fast. Then a couple of years later, my husband and I helped to sponsor *Yeay* Mao and her family. Like the three of us, Maly and Chandra grew up together. *Yeay* Mao and her husband won the lottery a couple of years ago. So they have a very nice house."

"You mean the *lottery* lottery?" I asked.

"Yes, the lottery."

"The millions-of-dollars lottery?"

"Oh, no. They won only a couple hundred thousand dollars. Now they have a big home for their daughter's wedding."

"I want to get married in a church," I said.

Chet pushed me lightly on the shoulder. "You're too young to think about that, kid."

"Really, Mr. I'm-Still-Only-Twenty?"

"It's in our culture to marry at home. I remember my wedding perfectly," *Oum* Palla said. "And you know what? I didn't know my husband until my parents said I was getting married."

I was appalled. "How can that happen?"

"Arranged marriages? That's how it usually happened. How do you think Maly and her fiancé met?" *Oum* Palla had said this so easily, like marrying someone you didn't know was the most logical thing in the world.

I still couldn't imagine marrying a total stranger. What if he was so short that I couldn't wear heels? "Weren't you scared?"

Oum Palla mulled my question. "A little, I guess. But I wasn't really worried about him. I worried about myself. I remember that the night before my wedding your grandma and I lay still on the floor. The hours were moving fast, and I felt this change in the air. So many things filled my head. I thought about my husband and me and how I would live with him and his parents and five brothers. I thought about the new house I would move into, the rules of it. And then I thought about leaving my parents. But what I thought about most was losing that moment—that exact moment I was living. Like there would be no other like it. Do you know what I mean?"

I told *Oum* Palla yes, remembering the nights Grandma and I had looked out our window. Most of those times, we didn't even speak to each other. When she knelt beside me and giggled, I was grateful to hear the soft purrs coming from her, thinking how rare those happy sounds were and knowing that in the next few seconds they would be gone.

"And what about my grandmother and grandfather? Was their marriage arranged, too?"

"You don't know?" she asked.

I shook my head, ashamed that strangers knew more

about my grandmother than I did. They were probably thinking that I hadn't cared enough about her to ask questions.

"No. Theirs was something different. They fell in love before they got married. He was a soldier. Very handsome."

I thought of my grandfather as a handsome soldier. Had that been the reason my grandmother was attracted to him? "What was he like?"

"Oh," she said slowly, "very strong." And just like that, she turned silent.

We'd walked down several blocks before we made another left turn. We passed a gated grassy area with a walking trail inside of it on the right-hand side. Across from the small park stood a wooden post that read Pleasant Lane.

I touched the orange and blue birds-of-paradise on either side of the wooden sign. The large houses here were two stories tall with fancy bay windows and French doors. Lights built into the ground highlighted various bushes and ficus plants.

We went up to the third house and rang the doorbell. After several minutes, *Yeay* Mao greeted us. She was a light-skinned, pudgy woman, about Grandma's height, with a man's haircut. Her face was full and very rosy. Hanging from her long earlobes were jade earrings the size of my thumbnails. She did not look Cambodian at all, but more Chinese. "So long," she greeted loudly in Cambodian. "What took you so long? Trying to look good, eh?" She chuckled.

"What else?" *Oum* Palla replied jokingly in Cambodian.

She, Chet, and I bent down to take off our shoes and placed them neatly next to each other against the wall of the foyer.

The inside of the house had clean white walls with cathedral ceilings in the two side-by-side living rooms. The floor was white ceramic tile with gray grout, and the carpet going up the stairs was light pink, almost the shade of my comforter back home.

"Here." *Oum* Palla showed the bag of fish to *Yeay* Mao. Then she said to her son, "Put this away for your grandma."

Chet took the bag and walked to the back of the house. "Good luck," he whispered behind me. I looked after him, wondering what he was talking about.

"What is this? Why did you bring it? You don't have to bring something every time. Don't do it again," *Yeay* Mao ordered.

"Okay, I won't," *Oum* Palla said, sounding as though she had said this before on each of her visits.

We went to the cream-colored sofas up front. Behind one of them was a long window, which was set off by two large houseplants. A tall vase of several lucky bamboos sat in the center of the glass coffee table. Every inch of the ceramic tile floor and every item in the house was freshly cleaned, and as I sat beside *Oum* Palla with my hands folded on my lap, I felt very small.

Yeay Mao pointed at me as she asked *Oum* Palla, "Who is this?"

"Who do you think? Take a guess," *Oum* Palla answered teasingly. "Look really hard. Who does she look like?"

Yeay Mao peered at me. "No way."

Oum Palla laughed. "Why 'no way'?"

Yeay Mao pursed out her bottom lip. "For real?"

"You ask her," *Oum* Palla answered.

For the first time that night, *Yeay* Mao paid me her full attention. "What's your name?"

My throat was dry, and it came out, "G-g-g-race."

"Grrr-eh?" she asked, which was as poor as Grandma's.

I shook my head. "No. Grace."

"Gr-race?"

I shook my head again. "Grace. *Graaace.* One syllable," I said in English, holding up one finger.

"Enough, enough." She waved her right hand at me. "Grrrace. Grace. G-race. It's just a name."

I bit my lip and sat up straighter.

"Who are you the child of?" *Yeay* Mao asked more gently. Her cheeks pushed up, and her eyes narrowed into slants.

I glanced at *Oum* Palla. "Chandra Hok."

"Chandra!" *Yeay* Mao screamed.

Oum Palla laughed. But I was scared. I was scared because I finally understood where I was: in a house belonging to a woman I didn't know, sitting beside another woman who I liked but didn't really know, in a city that I met just a day earlier. This was something I wanted, but at the same time I felt lost. Where were my father, my mother, and my grandmother to bridge me to all of these people and things?

Yeay Mao bent in closer to me. "Where's your dad?"

Where? I hated that question. I hated what the

interrogators thought once I answered "Not here" or "He's not around." I could see their eyes cutting me in halves, as though my lack of a father explained so much.

Before I could answer, *Oum* Palla spoke for me. "*Yeay,* you ask so many questions."

"You're Naree's granddaughter. For real," *Yeay* Mao said more calmly, to herself. "Look at her," she said to *Oum* Palla. "Looks just like Naree when she was younger. Before Pol Pot. Before her face changed." *Oum* Palla nodded. *Yeay* Mao clicked her tongue a couple of times, and turned somber. "Pol Pot changed everything."

Grandma had mentioned Pol Pot to me. People had died awful deaths during that time. Others had been born then. "Those Khmer Rouge men and women ate people's liver," she had said to me one afternoon when she was planting spearmint in a window box. I thought that she was hallucinating again. I believed in deaths and births, but I did not believe in people tearing up bodies like animals. That was dirty, embarrassing, and I hoped that none of my friends would ever think that Cambodians did something like that.

Yeay Mao exclaimed, "Where is Naree? Why didn't she come to see me? I haven't seen her in so long. Left and didn't call, didn't write. We came all the way from Cambodia together, and she departed like we didn't know one another. Huh? Where is your grandmother?"

"*Slab heiy,*" *Oum* Palla said regretfully. Passed away. "Chandra brought her ashes here for *bouhn.* We will have to do it this weekend."

"Not Saturday!" *Yeay* Mao exclaimed. *Oum* Palla told

101

her to calm down, that it would not be on Saturday but Sunday. *Yeay* Mao sucked in her breath and exhaled so loudly that I saw her belly rising and flopping like a deflated basketball. "So sad. Your grandma's life was so sad," she said to me, frowning, and then to *Oum* Palla, "Naree's dad cursed her forever. I told you that, didn't I? I told you when it first happened. What he did to her. Real fathers don't do that."

"What did he do?" I asked.

"In Cambodia? You don't know?" She slapped herself on the chest. "She never told you?" I kept still, afraid to answer her.

"Who wants to talk about things like that?" *Oum* Palla asked her friend. "People want to talk about happy things."

"What are you talking about?" she asked indignantly. "Children should know what their mothers went through. They should know so they will be grateful for their lives. If you don't tell them anything, then they think everything is so easy." In a softer voice she said to me, "You want to know? I'll tell you."

I nodded.

"Do you remember, Palla?" *Yeay* Mao asked. "It was the rainy season, right?" *Oum* Palla moved her head lightly in acknowledgment. "Your grandma was about eight or nine years old. Oh, she was wild. Walking around like she was one of the boys. Shooting marbles. Fishing. Climbing tall palms to pick coconuts."

It was strange for me to picture my grandmother doing these things.

"One night your grandma played outside in the rain

and wouldn't come inside, even after her dad had threatened to beat her. But your great-grandmother loved your grandma so much. She thought Naree was her great-uncle, you know?"

"Yes," I said, even though I didn't.

"She never raised her voice at Naree. She wouldn't let anyone say anything unkind to her, either. But your great-grandfather, her husband, was always jealous of the time and attention that she gave Naree. Well, that rainy night, all three of them were outside in front of their house. Houses weren't too far away from one another, so we could easily hear and see everything. I watched them from my house, which was high, because it stood on tall stilts. Your great-grandfather couldn't get Naree to come inside the house and he couldn't get his wife to do it, either. Oh, I remember the anger on his face. It was strange, but I could see him thinking. Like he was realizing how he could never get either his wife or daughter to listen to him. How some people were talking about him not being able to control either of them. Then . . . then . . . the next thing I saw was him pulling—in one swift motion—your grandma's sarong. He just pulled it off. And it lay around her ankles. And then!" *Yeay* Mao hollered at me as though I was the one in the wrong. "He pointed at your grandma and asked his wife if what was between Naree's legs was a dick. Now, what father does that? Shaming his own daughter?"

She peered at me for an answer, but the only thing I knew to do was to look up at *Oum* Palla and ask her if it was true. Because it was too awful for a father to do to his daughter.

"I wasn't there. I don't know," *Oum* Palla said.

Yeay Mao pointed a finger at her friend. "I know! I saw it. My house was across from hers. I saw everything." She turned to me. "Your grandma opened her mouth to scream, but no sound came out—she looked so scared. So betrayed! Even when her mom bent down to pull up her sarong. The humiliation. And that sight—" She sighed. "People can never forget."

"Stop it," *Oum* Palla said gently to *Yeay* Mao. She patted me on the back and told me, "It's okay."

"It's not okay," *Yeay* Mao said defiantly. "What her father did broke her." She placed her fists side by side and quickly dropped one of them. "He broke her future."

"Okay, okay," *Oum* Palla said. "That's enough. Stories that don't have use shouldn't be told. Now, what's going on with the wedding? When are the in-laws coming?"

"I'll tell you," *Yeay* Mao said. "First I need something to drink. I'm so thirsty."

"Because you talk too much." *Oum* Palla motioned me to follow her and *Yeay* Mao to the kitchen.

"Most of the time I don't talk as much as you," *Yeay* Mao retorted.

The kitchen looked like it had been taken straight out of a home magazine. Chet was sitting at the island and watching a sports show on a small television set. *Yeay* Mao took three short glasses from the dishwasher and filled them up with Minute Maid orange juice. We stood at the counter as the two women sipped their juice and continued to banter about who talked more. My mouth tasted sour, and I didn't think it was the juice. I couldn't erase the image of my grandmother standing in the rain with her skirt around her ankles.

"The in-laws are coming on Wednesday night. Cheaper tickets," *Yeay* Mao told *Oum* Palla. "Plus, they can't leave their jewelry stores. I just spent the day cleaning the house. So busy every day. No time to rest."

Oum Palla frowned. "You have it easy with three grown sons, already married with their own families, and a daughter. Maly's a good daughter. She can help you. What do I have? Two lazy sons. And what will I do once they get married? They're going to move away and be with their wives. It's not like Cambodia," she said.

I caught Chet watching me, and now understood why he had wished me luck.

Yeay Mao laughed at *Oum* Palla. "You don't know. It is tougher to raise a daughter than a son. Do you know how hard it is to be the mother of a daughter? You feel that you can't eat, can't sleep. Because all you do is worry about your daughter. How she turns out shows the world who you and your family are. Your daughter can't be anything but perfect. Because if she isn't, then she is very flawed, like a jewel dropped in mud. Then who would want to marry her? Who would want a dirty jewel?"

"Can't you just wash that under a faucet?" I asked.

Yeay Mao snapped a look at me, and *Oum* Palla told me to hush. "This is an adult conversation," she said.

Chet chuckled until his mom told him to shut up. If I could have done it without anyone noticing me, I would have flipped him off.

The two women continued to argue about sons and

daughters when the garage door opened. "My daughter is home," *Yeay* Mao said and clapped her hands under her chin. "Maly is home."

She, *Oum* Palla, and I put down our glasses and walked to a small, dark hallway on one side of the house, where we stood single file, as though to greet the president himself. There were the sounds of the car door opening, closing, the engine shutting off, and footsteps shuffling across the floor before the door to the house opened with a creak. A lady wearing a red beret and holding shopping bags in her right hand walked in, looking exhausted. As with her mother, she was light-skinned, like fine porcelain, and her hair, which she wore straight down her back, was long, a little reddish, and perfectly highlighted.

Yeay Mao took the bags from her daughter and asked how it all went. "Did the clothes fit the two girls? Were they happy with the colors we picked out?"

Maly walked ahead of us, and we followed her back to the kitchen, where she waved at Chet and went to the refrigerator for a bottle of Perrier. We stood around the island watching her drink from the green bottle, and I wondered if anyone was going to introduce me to her.

Maly told us about her awful evening with her junior bridesmaids. "Janet was fine," she said in Cambodian. "She wears only American clothes, so it was awkward to see her in the *phamourng* and *kben*. And she walked a little weird, too, in the *phamourng,* like her hip was out of joint. But that's not the problem. The problem is that the other girl, Elizabeth, fell while rollerblading and now has a twisted ankle."

"Mother!" *Yeay* Mao exclaimed in Cambodian. "What are we going to do?"

"I don't know," Maly cried. "But *Mak,* we can't have a crippled kid walk around in the wedding. It will look terrible in the video. She won't be able to sit down and get up off the floor gracefully. I can't believe this is happening."

Yeay Mao said, "Some people just don't think," and touched her daughter gingerly on the shoulder. "How are we going to find another girl her age at the last minute?"

"And comparable to Janet's size," Maly added. "I can't have one girl too short and the other too tall. Nothing will look uniform. Why now?" she whined.

I didn't know Maly, but I was sorry that she was having this problem when her special day was just around the corner. I didn't know Elizabeth or her mother, either, but I cursed them anyway for being so careless when they knew she would have to be in a wedding. I'd never been in a wedding, but I knew how important the position was. I used to envy the girls who brought in their flower girl bouquets for show-and-tell. If I'd been honored with the duty of being a junior bridesmaid, I would have taken great care of myself. I'd probably quit shaving just to save my legs from nicks.

"I am so sorry," I said. "But I'm sure everything will turn out just fine."

Maly finished the Perrier and studied me, her head tilted daintily. Instead of eyebrows, she had two blackish blue arches. There was a beauty mark above and to the right of her lips, although it was more like a heavy ink mark. She smiled and told me I was sweet, looking at me with that uncertain expression. I told her my name. "And you know my mom, Chandra," I said. "Do you remember her?"

It took her a couple of seconds to register what I'd just said, and then Chet explained, "You know, Chandra? Your best friend in school?"

"Ohhhhh," Maly said, less enthusiastic than I had expected. "Chandra. How is she? Where is she?"

I was about to fill her in when the front door opened. We all walked to the foyer. "What? How are you, *Bang* Palla?" the thin tall man warmly asked in Cambodian.

"Fine, Father of Maly," *Oum* said. "How are you?"

"Less tired if my wife didn't send me around town on so many errands." He took off his tennis shoes and handed his wife a department store bag. "She wants you to try it on. If you're still unhappy with it, she'll fix it again."

Yeay Mao mumbled under her breath as she pulled out an apricot-colored dress from the bag. She held it out for us to see: a straight line cut with a slit in the back. The material was the same as the Cambodian gowns that Grandma had hanging in Mom's closet. The hem of the skirt and the short sleeves were sewn with teardrop beads, the neckline was scalloped, and there was a fold down the front of the skirt. "Look at this. I am too old. How can she make the neckline so low? How can I wear it for my daughter's reception? People will think I'm competing with her."

Oum Palla laughed at this, and Maly's dad did, too. "Don't worry. No one will mistake you for our daughter," he said.

"She did it on purpose," *Yeay* Mao moaned. When her

husband didn't stop laughing, she slapped him on the back and took the dress with her up the stairs.

Maly's dad turned to me; his straight white hair came down to his earlobes. *Oum* Palla told him who I was, and he stepped back. "But you're such a big girl. How old are you? Twenty? Twenty-five?"

"No," I answered seriously.

"Oh," he said, nodding emphatically.

"Oh, you were joking!" Before I could give Maly's dad a real answer, I heard *Yeay* Mao coming back down the stairs.

"Father," she said crossly in Cambodian to her husband, "you always like to joke around. If you do it, make it somewhat real, won't you. Twenty. Does that child look twenty to you? Her mom had her as soon as she left here. That's what happens when a child doesn't listen to her mother," she added as she walked to the kitchen.

The house turned eerily quiet, as if what *Yeay* Mao had just said required a moment of silence so that everyone could fully understand how dire the situation was: I was the product of my mother not listening to her mother. I was beginning to understand why Mom hadn't wanted to come back to St. Pete. If *Yeay* Mao had asked me for my opinion, I would have told her that if she was right, then each girl at my school would be dropping a baby every five minutes.

Maly's dad excused himself, and I watched him go up the stairs. And *Oum* Palla pretended to study a framed picture of the White House. Chet shrugged, as if to say that that was how it was among these people.

We stayed in our own balloon of silence until Maly, who had been reading the mail at the dining room table, gasped for air, and we turned to see if she was choking. She pointed at me with a shaking finger. "How old are you? Huh? Huh? How old are you?"

Before I could answer her, *Yeay* Mao hurried toward her daughter. "She's only here for a week. For her grandmother's funeral."

Maly continued to point at me.

"Maly," *Yeay* Mao said firmly, "her grandmother just died. You can't ask her to do this."

"Fourteen," I said.

Maly walked to me with her arms open like she was Jesus embracing me. "You'll be perfect. You're about Janet and Elizabeth's size. You'll be perfect in my wedding. Oh, look at you. You're adorable." She reached out and squeezed my cheeks. "Do you want to be my bridesmaid?"

"Ah, I don't know."

"It will be fun. I have so many people coming. You'll be so beautiful. Everyone will see you."

So many people coming? I thought.

"*Coan,*" *Yeay* Mao said. "It's not good. She will be busy."

Yeay Mao pouted, her cheeks pudgier than ever. But at that moment I disliked her as much as I disliked pop quizzes. Besides, I was too shameless to care about her feelings. I was going to be a bridesmaid! "Do you mean it?" I asked Maly. "Really? I can be in your wedding?"

Maly hugged me. But as pretty as she was and as happy as I was to be in her arms, I couldn't help but notice the stench of her long, perfectly highlighted, unwashed hair.

I contemplated showing Chet the picture of my father when I asked, "Was what she said true? Was all of it true?" The night hadn't fully set in, but several stars had already begun to litter the sky, sparkling like bits of glass. Chet was walking me home because Nahrin had called earlier to say that he and Mom had gotten back. *Oum* Palla stayed with *Yeay* Mao to help with some of the wedding preparations.

"What are you talking about?" he asked.

"You know, what *Yeay* Mao said about my grand-mother and her dad. Was it true that he did that?"

"I don't know."

"But why would he embarrass his daughter like that? A father is supposed to protect you, pick you up, and show you to the world. He's supposed to say, 'Look, this is my beautiful daughter.' "

"Yeah, if you were the Lion King," Chet said. I rolled my eyes at him, and he rubbed me on the head. "Kid, I'm just saying that not all fathers are . . . I don't know . . . per-fect people. I mean mine was pretty cool. But not all of them are that way."

I pulled away from him. "I know that. I'm not stupid. I've seen the dads on *Law and Order.*"

Chet put up his hands. "Who said you're stupid? I'm just trying to tell you that—"

"Look, just because I don't have a father living with me doesn't mean that I don't know anything. Okay?"

"Okay."

111

We started walking again. "If it isn't true, then why would *Yeay* Mao say it?" I asked.

"Say what?"

"About my grandmother being her mother's great-uncle? It's all so weird."

"I don't know. I guess it's like with everything else. They just do. Just like what they said about your great-grandmother rolling an egg under your grandma's bed to end what she remembered about her past life."

I touched him on the arm. "What?"

"It's true. Believing something like that is common for us. You know, living, dying, and living again. That's why you'll see all the old Cambodians going to temple and praying all the time, to build up good karma. So they don't come back as . . ." He snickered. "As cows or caterpillars."

I knew about karma. Grandma had explained it to me. From what I understood, it was almost like the Ten Commandments to her. She said it was what kept people "good." Good people didn't kill animals just to see them suffer. Good people treated elders with respect. They gave food to the monks. They set up altars and placed food atop them as offerings to their ancestors. They did these things because they knew that they would die someday and be re-born again. And they wanted their new lives to be filled with riches, no suffering, no heartaches, only happiness, a lot of food, and good health.

"But what does that have to do with the egg?"

"When she was a little kid," Chet said, "your grandma talked a lot about people that she shouldn't have known about, people who . . . I don't know . . . lived when her mother's great-uncle was alive. And her mother said that she had never told your grandmother about them. So then people in their village began saying that in her previous lifetime, your grandmother was her mother's dead great-uncle. And your great-grandmother believed it. And that's why she spoiled your grandma. You know, she was afraid of mistreating her own great-uncle."

"So, what happened then, to my grandmother?" I asked.

"After what your great-grandfather did to her, your great-grandmother rolled an egg under her bed when she was asleep, and the next morning your grandmother woke up with no memory of her past life."

"What? That was all it took? An egg? To wipe out someone's memory?"

"I guess."

I wasn't sure if I believed Chet. And I didn't know if I wanted to. I once attended church with Tracy, and her pastor said that religions of the East were wrong and backward. I didn't believe him then, but walking with Chet that night, I wondered if the pastor had been right. And if he had been, then I didn't want him to be. I didn't want my grandmother to be more wrong and backward than she already was.

8

I shut off the light in our room and slipped under my pink comforter. Grandma had come to bed an hour earlier, and now she was snoring, a sound like a whistle. Across the short hallway, I heard Mom's feet moving in her room: she was walking to her tote bag to put away her students' papers, crossing over to her small bookcase to store the textbooks, and then to her closet to pick out tomorrow's outfit, which she would iron and rehang. Another day had come, and it was almost over. Nothing much had changed.

I was eight, and as I lay listening to these lonely, familiar sounds, I heard my father's car pulling up to our house and parking. I count to ten, and then I hear him opening the front door. Mom will have to wake up early tomorrow morning, so she cannot greet him. I get out of bed as quietly as I can, walking on my toes, open the bedroom door, and go down the dark stairway. The light is on in the kitchen, and Dad is in there, his head in the refrigerator.

"Mom left your dinner in the microwave," I say.

He turns around, a wide grin on his face, and opens his arms to me. His tie has come off, and the shirtsleeves are rolled up to his elbows. I run to him and hug him, and he is so big that my arms don't wrap around him completely. I smell sweat and cologne on his stomach, and I can't get enough of it.

"Long day at the office again," I say.

"Just a couple of more days, Gracie," he says.

I tell him that I understand.

He carries his plate of rice and chicken, and I carry his glass of water, and we walk together to the table.

"Shouldn't you be in bed, Gracie?" he asks.

"I can't sleep."

"You want to tell me about it?"

"Not really."

"Tell me."

I tell him about language arts class. "The teacher put all of us in groups. She put all of my friends together and left me out."

"Left you out how?"

"Out of the group. I'm in a different group."

"What's wrong with that?" he asks.

"All of my friends are together. They are going to have fun and tell each other stories."

"So? You can have fun and tell stories with people in your own group."

"It's not the same," I explain. "They're going to work together, even going to each other's houses, and they might not invite me."

"That could be the case," he says.

I don't like his response and cry, "I don't want to lose my friends."

"If they're your friends, Gracie, you're not going to lose them."

I smile at him. He always knows what is wise and true. He smiles back, forgetting his dinner.

"Tell me about your day," I say.

"Oh, it was tiring. I had to think all day," he says.

"What about?"

He winks at me. "You."

I smile at him again, but this time his head is faced down as he finishes the last piece of chicken. I reach my hand into the fruit basket, grab a red apple, and polish it with a napkin. He will want it for dessert. . . .

Mom's feet stopped moving, and her bed creaked. I briefly pictured her in her bed, the soft sheets warming her. She'd close her eyes, and soon, like Grandma, she'd fall asleep. And as I listened to her sound and Grandma's, I would keep making up stories about my father, and I would not know I'd shut my eyes until I woke up the next morning.

My mother was sitting across from me, shaking her finger in a "no" after I told her about the visit to Maly's house.

"No? Why can't I be in the wedding?" I asked as I picked up a longan.

When Chet and I had returned to his house, Mom and Nahrin were sitting at the dining table. Rolling around like marbles on the table, which was completely covered with newspaper, were brown-looking nuts that Nahrin said were longans. He handed one to me, and I took the strange-looking fruit from him. I watched as he picked up one for himself, broke the soft shell open with his teeth, and sucked the white meat out, spitting the brown-black seed onto the newspaper.

As I waited for Mom to answer me, Chet busily popped the longans like peanuts. Mom concentrated on the fruit, too, swaying gently.

"Why can't I be in *Bang* Maly's wedding?" I asked again. "She was your friend."

"We didn't come here for a wedding. Besides, it's not what it's cracked up to be," she said.

How would you know? I thought, remembering the photo Grandma had shown me of her crying.

"Some Cambodians are very strict when it comes to weddings," Nahrin said. He was staring at me intently, as though he was waiting for me to say that I understood. But I didn't, so he leaned into the table and folded his hands, like Mom sometimes did, and went on, "They think every aspect of that ritual affects their children's future. Some people even pick one day over another because they think one day is luckier."

"So? What does that have to do with bridesmaids?"

"Like your mom said, it won't be that fun. There will

be a lot of work. You'll be tired. I agree with her." Nahrin smiled, seeming satisfied. What had he and Mom talked about that caused him to think he could speak to me this way?

Chet got up from the table and said he had to call his girlfriend. Mom sat back in her chair, seeming relieved that the discussion was over. Actually, she seemed thankful that Nahrin had enlightened me! I didn't know what was going on. Earlier in the day, *Oum* Palla's presence had silenced her, and now Nahrin was speaking for her? It was truly uplifting to see that my mother could go speechless and be taken down from her throne of command, but I didn't need for her to sit back and let an old flame of hers speak to me as though he had a right to.

I stood taller than I had ever done before. "I'm sorry," I said to Nahrin. "I mean this in the most polite way. But I don't care what you think. You're not my father."

Mom kept her face down, and Nahrin's head rested on the wall, his eyebrows raised up into his forehead. I didn't wait for either him or my mother to say anything as I walked out.

It was well past midnight when Mom came to bed. After I left her and Nahrin, I remained in our bedroom, not knowing what to do. I was not sorry that I had told Nahrin to mind his own business. Who did he think he was to agree with Mom, like he was her second half? Did he think I would care? But I was sorry that Mom had heard me.

While I sat alone, I hated the small room. I hated

how there was no space to move around in. I hated the grotesquely large fan that was hanging above the bed. And the bed that had a dead mattress. Who keeps a bed with no freakin' support? But what I hated most was Mom and these strangers who weren't supposed to be strangers. These people who understood her, who could speak for her. More than I ever would. These people owned what was supposed to be mine, the days my grandmother and mother had lived. The days I was never told about.

Mom climbed into bed without turning on the lights. She did it so carefully that I didn't even feel a brush of her hand. Even in the full-size bed, there was a wide gap in between us, for everything we were unsure of; I am certain of this. I don't remember ever sharing a bed with her before then. It had always been Grandma who held me when I had the flu or a tummyache. And as much as I wanted to feel my grandmother's touch that night, I shut my eyes tight and bit into the sheet, doing all I could to not roll over to my mother and feel her warmth. There was nothing I wouldn't have given to have her pull me up against her chest and let her heart beat against my back.

"I'll apologize to him tomorrow," I said, my heart starting to race as I prepared for a lecture.

I felt her moving onto her side. "That would be good."

And? What else? Come on, give it to me now. I don't want to wait until morning. She didn't say anything, though.

"I thought you didn't want to come back here," I said.

She adjusted her pillow and mumbled, "What are you talking about?"

I flipped to my other side. Through the window, the

moon cast a soft beam of light across her face. "Remember? Your fights with Grandma? She wanted to move back here, but you said no. I wanted to come here, and you said no. Now you're all happy-go-lucky. You're not even stressed out about your lesson plans." *And you act like you like me,* I wanted to add.

"He wants us . . . the two of us . . . to stay here . . . in St. Pete," she said dreamily. "*Bang* Nahrin asked me to marry him."

I sat up. "What? We just got here. What about my dad? I can't believe—"

"I told him no," she said quickly, like that was the answer to everything I didn't understand.

In the moonlight, I could see the corners of her lips moving up, forming dimples in her cheeks. I was furious that she could smile when I was fuming.

I climbed over her and off the bed. I turned on the light, and she jolted up.

"What are you doing?" she whispered. There was nervousness in her voice—she was afraid that we were going to wake up *Oum* Palla, whose bedroom was directly across the hall from ours.

"How long have you and . . . and *Bang* Nahrin been . . . you know . . . hot for each other?" I asked calmly, even though I really wanted to scream.

"What?"

"You know, were you fooling around with him when you were with my dad? Was that why Dad didn't want to marry you?"

Mom shook her head at me like I was nuts. But I knew

I wasn't nuts. How could I be the nut when I wasn't the one who had changed all of a sudden? I was the same as I'd always been, wanting what I'd always wanted. She got out of bed and headed toward me, but I blocked the light switch. I could see the rising and falling of her chest. "Grace, this isn't the time or place."

Before, when she spoke to me with her steady and careful words, I wouldn't know what to say; I'd be so confused, and so frustrated at the fact that I was mad but she wasn't. I would search my brain for the right words to lash out at her with. Just to try to make her understand. But I would always turn up empty. So I would stand before her, a reprimanded child, forgetting who I was. Forgetting that I had created a rocket that flew fifty feet or that I had scored a perfect 100 on my multiplication test, the only one to do so in the class. Instead, I would go back to being four years old, still practicing the alphabet over and over so that I could recite it flawlessly for her, still throwing tantrums and then later mumbling that I was sorry.

But that night I remembered that I was a fourteen-year-old who didn't know her father, the person who made up half of who she was. And I remembered that my grandmother had just died. I remembered, too, the times I had slept at Tracy's house, the constant noise and chaos of her baby sister crying, her older stepbrothers threatening to beat her up, her aunts calling repeatedly to check on Sunday dinner, and her stepdad just lying on the couch reading a newspaper. Tracy did not want to be associated with her family, and she told me I was lucky to be an only child, to have peace and quiet. What she didn't know—and I didn't think she ever would—was how important it was that those people shared their blood with her, and that that would never change. All I wanted that night, as I stood in front of my mother, was to know whose blood I shared.

"Really?" I said. "Do you think the time and place was back at our house, then?" She didn't answer. "I agree. I think the time and place was back at our house. You know, where normal things are supposed to happen. But you forgot to share it with me then."

My mother's face turned blank. She walked to the bed and sat on the edge of it and wrapped a hand across her mouth, staring at the closet door.

"I'm sorry," I said quickly. And I was. Muting my mother wasn't as exhilarating as I had thought. "It's just that you've been acting strange. Like you're this laid-back person. Why couldn't you be more like this back home?"

"I don't know what to say," she said apologetically.

"I mean, I'm glad that you're not crying anymore. But you just sat there and let *Bang* Nahrin . . . He is not my dad."

"I know that you might not like him, but he had nothing to do with your dad." Keeping the rest of her body still, she turned her face to me. To this day I remember that pose clearly, her gentle, glowing face anchored by her bare shoulder. "Grace, do you remember a long time ago when you said that I keep you and your grandma safe? Well, *Bang* Nahrin and his mom did that for me. And I miss that. I miss having someone share my thoughts. Having someone speak for me. Sometimes I got so tired of having to speak for your grandmother."

I remembered all the translating Mom had had to do for her mother. I had thought that she liked making all the choices—exuding her power. But maybe it was a tiresome job?

"I didn't know," I said.

"It's okay. I didn't want you to worry about me. Your grandma and you—"

"I'm sorry," I said, knowing what she was trying to say. My grandmother and I were a team, and our shared opponent was my mother. I felt sorry for Mom, but it was her fault. She was the one who didn't come to see if I was okay. She was the one who hid herself in her bedroom.

"Don't get me wrong. I was happy that your grandma loved you. And that you loved her. I don't know if you'll ever understand, but it made it easier for me—for her to have someone else in her life."

"Then why were you always so angry with her? She's gone, and you still sound so angry, Mom."

She chuckled to herself. "Your grandma expected me to be perfect. And I simply wasn't."

"She did think you were perfect."

"Not really."

"Well," I said, "it's tough trying to be perfect."

Mom stared at me, and I had to turn away. "I never want you to feel that way. Grace, I never said you have to bring home straight As or that you have to dress a certain way. I give you freedom to be yourself."

It was true. I had to give my mother that much credit. As long as it was within the school's Code of Conduct, I could wear anything I wanted to school. She hadn't even given me a hard time for not drawing my family tree in the second grade. But I couldn't forget the times when she had told me how to order my food.

"So, getting pregnant with me made you imperfect."

She didn't say anything, and in that silence I realized how different, how wonderfully different, her life would have been for her if she and my father had never met. As much as you fight things sometimes, you always know the truth. I knew that my mother loved me, simply because she was my mother. Like Grandma had said, Mom bought me clothes and gave me lunch money. But I began to understand why she chose to be alone some days. Maybe on those days, she could pretend that she had never met my father and fallen in love with him, even for a short time. Maybe she could pretend that she and Grandma weren't in Scottsville. She would be here in St. Pete with Nahrin, probably married with three kids and a house painted yellow.

Mom said in a faraway voice, "I went to the prom with Maly. Nahrin asked your grandma if he could take me, but she said no, and I was livid. I didn't really know your dad when he walked up to me that night. He didn't go to our school, but I'd seen him around temple. So I knew a little bit about him."

I sat on the floor, my legs folded, picturing my father walking up to a girl from across a crowded room. "That's sweet."

"Your dad and I started to talk. He was nice. He told me I was pretty and smart. I guess the usual things guys say to girls. I knew he was hitting on me, but I didn't care. At that moment, I just wanted to be like most of my friends, someone who didn't care so much what her mom thought or wanted.

"Later he told me that he hadn't eaten and asked if I was hungry. I wasn't, but I said yes. He and I left the dance and got into his car, and we drove to a McDonald's drive-thru. Ordinarily I would have never done something like that, but that night I didn't care. Then we went down to the Pier and found a quiet place to park. He rolled down the window, and we listened to the waves spilling in on the sand, and we smelled the salty sea. And for a while, we just ate chicken nuggets and looked out at the black water.

"When I finished my box of nuggets, your father took it from me and threw it to the backseat. Then I grabbed his hand. Again, something I would have never done. Until then, Nahrin's hands were the only hands I had touched—when we were alone in the kitchen or at the side of the house. For a while your dad and I sat holding hands. Then he scooted in closer to me, and I knew he was too close when I smelled barbecue sauce on his lips. I could have told him to stop and to return to his own seat or to take me back to the dance, but that night I was so angry with your grandmother I was about to implode. *Bang* Nahrin and I were in love. She knew this. But it didn't seem to matter to her. She was so afraid of the community talking. I had always listened to her and believed her, but that night I didn't care anymore about that community. So I didn't tell your father to stop. And for the rest of that night, I didn't tell him to stop with anything."

As I waited for the rest of the story, I realized that my throat had become dry. And when it dawned on me, finally, that my mother wasn't going to go on, I asked, "Okay, then what happened?"

"And then you came along," she simply said, like that alone explained why I hadn't met my father, why she hadn't wanted to return to St. Pete, why Nahrin had just proposed to her.

"Then why did you and Dad break up?"

Mom did not answer me. And I understood then that she and my father were never together to begin with—that their lovemaking had been one big mistake. I'm not sure when the warmth and heat seeped out of me. I just know that I suddenly felt cool. I pulled my T-shirt down to cover my thighs.

She broke out in one of those quick, nervous, cheery grins, a sight I had grown to detest.

"Where is my father?" I asked.

"Grace—"

"Mom, please, where is he?"

"He's gone," she said.

"Stop saying that." I fought to make my voice heard. "Gone where?"

"Grace . . ." There was pain on her face, and I could only imagine my grandmother going through the same discomfort as she struggled before her fatal heart attack. "Your father's dead. He drowned."

The cold in that guest room found its way to my bones. I got up off the floor, dizzy. "No, he's not dead. How can you say that?" As I asked her these questions, I couldn't fight off the images of my grandmother with the sarong around her ankles. My dad sinking. "You're lying."

"I'm not. I've been trying to tell you. But you wouldn't listen."

"You did *not* try to tell me." I knew *I* was lying as I said those words to her. She was right. She'd always said that my father was "gone" and "he is not coming back." *It's not my fault for not believing you*, I wanted to tell her. "How do you know he drowned?" I whimpered.

"I wrote one of my high school teachers once. A long time ago. She wrote back and told me about a Cambodian drowning at the beach. She mentioned the name."

"It's not 'the name.' It's my father's name, Mom, something I don't even have."

"I know."

That was all she said.

There had to be more.

I reached out my hands and yanked the sheets from the bed with all my strength. Mom jumped. The mattress spring bleated and cried as I dragged the sheets off the bed. How could she be so calm when my insides were melting? My dad and I deserved more! I continued to grab the sheets and the blanket until everything was on the floor.

"Grace," she said, surprised.

"I hate this bed!"

Her eyes widened and were stunned, and for a quick moment I was glad that maybe she was afraid of me. "Grace, you wanted to know."

"No!" I remember that I wasn't angry that my father was completely and totally gone from this world, but that my mother hadn't been lying all this time. *He's gone!*

A knock at the door made me jump. I had forgotten that we were not in Scottsville.

Mom got up from the bed and cracked the door open, saying, "I'm sorry. Everything is okay." She closed the door, and I sat on the sheets.

The night outside was so still and quiet that the weight of it began to hurt my ears. I held a pillow to my stomach. "Did he know about me? Please tell me that he did."

She walked to her purse and pulled out a pen and a piece of paper, wrote something, then handed the paper to me.

Lee Hang. My father's name.

I studied the seven letters. "This is all I have of him."

"I called him when you were about one. He wanted to see you, but I told him no."

I saw my father holding me, both arms raising me high. "Why?"

Mom shrugged. "I don't know. I guess I didn't want him to talk me into coming back here."

I shook my head at her, not understanding. "He would have married you. Then you would have a husband. I would have a dad. And Grandma would have her friends. We would all be happy."

"But I didn't want a husband, not that way."

"It's always about you. Why couldn't you love me enough to make it about me?"

A deep wrinkle formed on her forehead. "I should have let him see you. I know. I'm sorry."

✖ ✖ ✖

Once Mom and I remade the bed, I crawled into it and lay on my side, and I looked at the window. I thought I would cry for my father's death, but I didn't. And I knew why. Somewhere within me, somewhere that I didn't want to pick at, I'd always known that he was gone from this world. Until tonight, my mother, maybe because she had wanted to protect me, just couldn't come up with those words: "he's dead."

But I had known.

9

In the living room, the blinds were opened and pulled to the side so that the morning light shot in like something fierce. *Oum* Palla was sitting on the leather sofa, and in front of her on the floor was a laundry basket filled with white candles, a large spool of white thread, and long bunches of fresh baby's breath.

I thought she would ask about the noises in our room last night, but instead she only said, "Did you sleep well?" I scratched my lower back and told her yes.

"Kids, especially young girls in Cambodia, don't sleep until the sun shines on their behind," she said in Cambodian. I didn't know what that meant exactly, but I had a pretty good idea that it was not a compliment.

I told her "Sorry," and she said that she was just telling me about the culture. "Take whatever I say that you like and throw out the rest. Okay, *Coan*?" Then she told me to come and sit with her.

I sat cross-legged beside the basket and asked where everyone was.

"Nahrin and your mom went to buy some clothes for you and herself. We will go to the temple later today to help with some things. And I think Chet is somewhere with his girlfriend again."

I yawned, fingered the candles in the basket, and asked what she was doing.

"Stuff for the funeral. People will carry these as we say nice things about your grandma and think about her." As she held up a bundle of three candles and a couple of flowers that were all tightly bound by thread, I wondered what nice things were said about my father at his funeral.

"They're very pretty. Is it true that my grandmother needs a Cambodian funeral so that she doesn't starve?"

Oum Palla tilted her head, seeming to think. "Don't Christians believe that Jesus will save them and take them to heaven?"

I pictured the white-garbed Jesus taking each person by the hand as they entered the gates of heaven together. "I guess."

"Well, *Coan*, as Khmer . . . we're on our own. When you leave this world, no Jesus is going to come along to hold your hand and walk you to heaven. Life and death are not that simple."

"Huh?"

"As a Buddhist, Grace, you can depend on only

yourself, and what your family and friends do for you after you die. Most of us die and are reborn into our next lives easily; some of us even go to nirvana. But a couple of us get lost. We can get stuck, you know what I mean? So we need help. If you have good karma, it's not too bad. Your next life and the road to it will be easy. But if you have bad karma, then you better pray that your children will give you a big funeral with everything imaginable to help make your travel better." *Oum* Palla smiled at me. "What did you have at your grandma's funeral in Scottsville? Flowers?"

I remembered the white plastic-looking carnations. "Yes."

"Flowers aren't going to help your grandma much. We need to give her money, food, and clothes."

I was wondering about the businesses operating on the road to nirvana when she asked if I had more questions. I told her no, deciding that I would never understand what she was talking about until I saw a Cambodian funeral in person. I was not sure which funeral I would want for myself, American or Cambodian. But from what I knew about Jesus, I thought it would just be easier to ask him for assistance.

Oum Palla said that I could help by handing her three candles at a time, but to make sure they were arranged to look like a pyramid. She showed me how the three white wicks at the top were supposed to form the points of an equilateral triangle. Ten sets of candles had been completed, and they were lined up on the glass coffee table like a picket fence.

"Are you okay with *Bang* Chet having a girlfriend?" I asked.

"Yes, I am."

"My grandma didn't even like it when I talked to a boy on the phone."

"I can see that about her."

Oum Palla was a smart woman, so I knew that after meeting me she must have known that Mom and Grandma left St. Pete because Mom was pregnant. I wonder, though, if she thought it had been the right decision. "I don't get it. Why is it okay that *Bang* Chet has a girlfriend, but girls can't have boyfriends?"

"It's the culture," she said.

"The culture?"

She nodded. "It's what we've grown up with."

I told her that the culture was unfair, and she told me that she agreed. She also explained that a person had to evolve with the changes, or she would have a hard time living a happy life. "Sometimes you have to move with the current, and not against it. But it's not easy to do, and most of us old folks usually fail at it."

"Do you miss Cambodia?" I asked.

"Of course, I miss the big temples there. But I really miss what the country was like before the war. The war killed so many things, not just the people." She gazed wistfully down at me as she held the candles I'd given her. "You know, I didn't speak to my husband after my parents and little brothers died? I blamed him that my parents' house was blown up." *Oum* Palla began to bind more candles. "I didn't speak to him for almost a year, not until I saw your grandmother again. Sometimes I wish that I could have those days, those months back, just so I could fill them up with words of how wonderful I thought he was, and not feel that my life will be cut short because I didn't."

"I'm so sorry," I said.

Oum Palla exhaled deeply, as though she'd kept something lodged in her chest for the longest time. She looked at me with wet eyes. "It was just that when my family died, I thought I had betrayed them. I was so angry that the Americans dropped those bombs on their home. I remember thinking that I didn't even repay my parents. I never cared for them during their old age. *Kaus khyal* them. Feed them. Massage them. Bathe them."

"When did you see my grandmother again?"

"A couple of years before the fall of the capital." Quietly *Oum* Palla placed three more candles on her lap and gingerly bound a long thread around them. Her fingers worked like chopsticks attempting to grasp noodles. After several minutes of trying, she said, "Grace, can you sit here? I need help tying this."

When I sat beside her on the sofa, she held the candles and baby's breath in a bundle while I wound and wound the long white thread about them. Once I made the knot, she held up the candles to me for closer examination. The knot in the thread was so tiny and tight that it could hardly be found.

Oum Palla began to work on some more candles. "I did this exact thing for my family's funeral."

I thought about the day Mom had picked out Grandma's funeral clothes. She didn't know what to send Grandma out of this world in: her working clothes, to signify how hardworking she was, her black *sapot* and the plain white button-down shirt she wore when she meditated on holy days, or the blueberry-colored sleeveless dress she'd bought and never worn. It was the only article she'd ever purchased at full price. Later, as Mom stood staring at the three outfits on Grandma's bed and finally chose the *sapot,* I thought it was so unfair for her to have to dress her mother for the last time. Wasn't it hard enough for her to say good-bye?

"That must have been awful," I said.

"It was awful. But it had to be done. What was worse, though, was that I thought I had lost everyone. And when you feel that way, you see yourself so alone. That everyone around you is ganging up on you. Your grandmother wasn't there, either. She and her mother had left to live in a different village."

"Why did they move?"

Oum Palla whispered in Cambodian, "You're still too young to have your day month. Right?"

I moved closer and whispered in her ear, "Actually, I'm not. I started my period—"

She held up her hand. "Kids in America grow up so fast."

I took our newly wrapped candles and placed them on the table.

"Well, at the time, Naree was a teenager. Sixteen. She was at a prime age for marriage—"

"Sixteen! A prime age to get married? And you think I'm too young!"

Oum Palla shushed me. "You don't understand, Grace. Back then if you were twenty and weren't married, then you could be thought of as an old maid."

"That's tough," I said, thinking that I would have only another six years before I was doomed for the nunnery if I were in Cambodia. Then it hit me. "If my grandmother was ready to get married when she was sixteen, then isn't *Bang* Maly kinda old?"

Oum Palla didn't answer right away; it was one of those pauses you knew were meant to be polite. "A little. Things are different now. Anyway, your grandma was ready for marriage, but no one was interested. There was always someone in our village who brought up the story of what had happened to her on that rainy night. So your great-grandmother felt that the only way for her daughter to have a future was to move them to a new town where, hopefully, those people wouldn't judge Naree for her father's act."

I pictured my grandmother as a little girl, her tender private area so bare and naked, in front of everyone to see. "That's so unfair."

"It was. As much as kids are a reflection on their parents, parents are also a reflection on their kids. And the children have to bear the burden longer. It walks with them everywhere, for the rest of their lives.

"After your grandmother left, I didn't see her for almost two years, not until we all migrated to Phnom Penh for safety. By this time, the Khmer Rouge and the Lon Nol government were in a full civil war, and the Khmer Rouge was gaining strength. All of us who lived in small villages were moving to the capital to get away from them."

"So, did it help that my grandmother and her mother moved away? Did she get married?"

Oum Palla smiled warmly at me. "Yes. When I saw Naree again, she was married to your grandfather and was pregnant with your mom. I already had Nahrin. Like some single young men, your grandfather was a soldier. And he was a nice-looking young man with a very short haircut and a pointy chin. His eyes turned inward slightly, though, so you were really looking at his nose bridge instead of his pupils. Your grandfather was a very nice man, Grace, and your grandparents were very much in love."

I could imagine my grandmother during those times, when my grandfather was alive. I could hear her soft giggles, the same ones I had heard when she and I sat at our window.

"After your mom was born and about a year later in Phnom Penh, your grandmother became pregnant again. And your grandfather had gone to battle. Oh, Naree was so devastated. The war was getting worse and worse. And a month before the fall of the capital, in 1975, your grandmother fell on the balcony of our apartment. My husband took her to the hospital, and they tried to save her baby. It was very sad, Grace, but when they cut her open the baby was already dead."

"She had another baby?"

"A baby girl," *Oum* Palla said.

I shut my eyes to block out the image of my

grandmother, her wide-opened stomach, and her bloody dead baby. But it only made me see more blood, the thickness and brightness of it spilling all over my vision. "I saw the scar on her stomach a couple of times, but no one told me about another baby."

Oum Palla picked up the candles again. "Like I said, some people can't talk about certain things in their pasts. Acknowledging them brings back pain they worked hard to bury."

I was sure she was right, but I didn't think it could be that simple. There had been a baby. A girl. She had fingers and toes, and tiny lips that I would be so scared to touch for fear of hurting her. She had existed. She was my aunt.

"Then what happened? Did my grandfather come back?"

Oum Palla gazed at me again, her eyes adjusting to seeing me, like she was just recognizing who I was. Then she plucked off a sprig of the baby's breath and aligned it with the candles on her thighs. "No, he didn't. We never saw him again. The Khmer Rouge came into Phnom Penh and ordered all of us out of the city and into the countryside. For four years they separated us and worked us without feeding us. Your grandma had it bad. The burn . . ."

Oum Palla sighed, and her mouth opened and closed suddenly. Her eyes had reddened, and her nose was shiny. I felt my chest tightening, and quickly I looked down at my lap, fidgeting with the candles. I thought back to the day that Grandma had told me about the Khmer Rouge eating human livers.

If I were braver, I would have said to *Oum* Palla, *Finish the story. Tell me how my grandmother got the scar on her face.* But in her moment of hesitation, I thought of my mother and her wish for freedom, and I began to understand that words about the past were like threads of a spiderweb: delicate, complicated, sticky, and even fatal. Did I really want to hear them and risk feeling stuck like my mother?

I chickened out, and said to *Oum* Palla, "My grandma made it out of Pol Pot like you, huh?"

Oum Palla patted me on the arm. "She did."

And that was all either of us said for the rest of the afternoon, which was fine with me. No matter how hungry you are, you can only eat so much until you are full.

I was studying page three of the temple directory when Chet came home and dropped his cell phone and keys on the dining table. I had gone through the directory five times already, one page at a time. Each time, it looked the same: a clean beige sheet of paper with neatly typed squiggly marks.

"What are you doing with that?" Chet asked. He was wearing a white undershirt and some running pants, and I could smell shampoo on him.

"Nothing," I said.

He rubbed me on the head, grabbed a soda from the fridge, and went to the sunroom. I heard him surfing the channels. He listened to a full beer commercial before he found a channel that satisfied him.

"Come here, Grace," he said. "Jack is on. It's really funny."

I took the directory and walked to the sunroom. Chet was watching a rerun of *Three's Company.* Jack was trying to steal back an expensive jacket Chrissy thought he'd given her. My grandmother had loved Chrissy. "That girl laughs like a pig," she would say.

Chet pointed to the end of the sofa. "Do you like this show?"

I kept the directory behind me as I sat down. "It's all right. But my grandmother liked it. She watched it non-stop, especially when there was a marathon on cable."

Chet slapped his thigh. "Ha-ha. Every Cambodian from your grandma's generation loves Jack."

"You mean John Ritter?"

"No. I mean Jack. If you ask any of them, no one will know who John Ritter is. But if you say Jack, they'll know exactly who you're talking about. Even if he starred in a different show, they would point to him and say 'Jack, Jack.' Hell, I think my mom cried the day he died."

I recalled that day, too. When Mom told Grandma the news, she was so flabbergasted. "A big movie star like him. He died?" Grandma asked.

"Well, my grandmother liked that *Knight Rider* dude, too," I said. "She watched him whenever the show was on. She didn't believe me when I told her that the stupid car didn't really talk."

"Oh, I'm sure she liked Hasselhoff. She probably liked *Magnum, P.I.,* too."

I moved in my seat. "Yeah! That's how I started to know about Tom Selleck. There was a rerun one day, and I watched it with her. I like him the best, of those three men. You know, he seems to be the smartest. The coolest. The most sophisticated. I know everything about him."

Chet laughed at me.

"What?"

"Nothing."

"You don't believe me? Come on, ask me a question." He shook his head. "Come on. Anything."

"Okay," Chet said. "How many kids does Selleck have?"

"Two. A daughter and a son. The son, from his first marriage and whom he adopted, is Kevin. And the daughter, from his second marriage, is Hannah. Come on. Another one. Something harder."

"How many movies has he been in?"

"Twenty-four movies and twenty-five television shows, and that doesn't include *Friends,* in which he played Monica's boyfriend. And he's been playing this police guy name Jesse Stone on TV. Another one."

Chet brushed me off. "Okay. Okay. You know everything about Selleck. But don't you think he's a little old for you to have a crush on?"

My cheeks burned. "I don't have a crush on him." Chet didn't seem to believe me. "Look, Tom Selleck doesn't take crap from anyone, okay? He drives his red Ferrari fast, but he always catches the bad guy, and he is honorable."

"You mean Magnum is."

I rolled my eyes and sat back in the sofa. "I mean Magnum."

"I got one for you," he said. "Do you know why old people like Jack the best?"

"No," I answered. Who cared about Jack? He was a clown who was obsessed with sex.

"They understood him."

"I don't get it," I said, annoyed at his know-it-all-ness.

"It's easy. With *Three's Company,* old people don't have to understand a single word Jack is saying. He's tripping all the time and making those ridiculous faces. They understand him. It's easy for them. They don't have to know English to appreciate American TV." He paused. "What are you doing with the directory?"

I didn't realize that I had moved it to my lap, and put my hands on it. "Nothing."

Jack, Chrissy, and Janet started to pull on the jacket in three different directions. Chet laughed. "This show is so stupid, but damn, it's funny." He glanced at me. "You were pretty mad last night, huh?"

I stiffened. "I'll apologize to your brother. I'm sorry. I didn't mean to get all rude in your house."

"Ah, we don't care."

I watched Chet watching the show, the constant grin on his face. A couple of times he hit a pillow as he roared with laughter. *He really doesn't care that I was disrespectful to his brother,* I thought.

"How did your dad die?" I asked.

"Stroke."

"Do you miss him?"

"Yeah. Some days more. Some days less. But every day."

"I'm sorry." *I'm sorry.* People, I was beginning to

142

understand, say these two words because they can't do anything else to relieve you of your pain.

"Yeah. Thanks."

"This thing?" I held up the directory, but Chet was watching TV again. "This?" I said again, and he looked over. "I can't read it."

"I know. It's written in Cambodian. Why do you need to read it?"

"I don't know. I just thought that maybe, you know, I could . . ." I took a deep swallow. "My dad died, too. He drowned."

Chet turned off the television, faced me, and folded his legs on the couch. "Oh. Sorry, kid."

I shrugged. "At least I know now."

"When did it happen?"

"My mom said about eleven years ago."

"Are you okay?"

How does a person answer that? But remembering that Chet had lost his father, I figured that he had the right to ask. "I don't know. I guess so. I think that my mom has been wanting to tell me, and she finally did last night. It's just that now it's . . . pretty final, you know? Like there is no sense of hoping now." Or dreaming. "It's weird to know that he and my grandmother will never come back."

"It must be tough, what you're going through."

My eyes began to sting, and I pushed back my tears. I wasn't as successful with the lump in my throat. "Do you think it was hard . . . the way he died?"

It took a while for Chet to say "I don't know." I appreciated his honesty.

"I was in the room when my grandmother died. My dad . . . he must have been alone. He must have been so scared. I can't imagine dying alone."

"I'm sure he was a good guy. I'm sure he's living a happier life now."

I nodded, holding up the directory again. "I would like to look for his family."

Chet opened his mouth and hesitated. "Did you talk to your mom about what you want?"

I said with finality, "No. And I'm not going to."

"But—"

"I'm not going to." I knew that my mother was sorry that she hadn't let my father visit me, but I didn't know how she would feel about me searching for his relatives. And I couldn't take the chance of her fighting me about it. "I don't have much time. I'm going to find them. It would be easier for me if you help me. Please."

Chet reached out to touch my hand. "I would help you, kid, but I can't read Cambodian, either."

I sat up. "But you can still help me."

"Huh?"

"You know people here. You can ask around."

Chet put up his hands and shook his head. "Oh, no. I'm not starting any problem."

"What are you talking about?"

"You want me to ask people about your dad and his family, and they'll start talking about your mom."

I rolled my eyes at him. "What is the big deal? What is there to talk about? Don't you think people will see her and me at my grandma's funeral and add up all the numbers and know that she had premarital sex? You knew. Your mom and *Bang* Nahrin, too. Even nasty old *Yeay* Mao knew."

"Still. If your mom or my mom find out about this, they're going to kick my ass."

"No one's going to kick your ass. I just want an address. That's all."

Chet shook his head emphatically.

"My dad is gone. My grandmother, too." I sucked in my lips, feeling the lump in my throat expanding. "My mom said that I have to leave my grandmother here on Sunday. I can't leave this place without taking something back with me. If I can't have my dad, I should get to at least have his family. That's only fair."

"But even if I try, I don't know if I can help you," Chet said.

I knew that was possible. But I was willing to take that chance. "You can ask questions, you know? You can even do it on the down low, like Magnum. Please, *Bang* Chet."

Chet stared at the TV screen for so long I thought he'd forgotten about me. Then he ran his hand through his wavy hair. "No one will know we're doing this?" he asked. I shook my head. "I don't want people to start giving your mom a hard time, okay?" I nodded. "So we do this quietly, and we do this my way?"

"Yes."

"Fine, kid," he said. "What's your dad's name?"

At the temple later that day, the music was turned up high again, and people stood outside in groups, working

145

on different projects. A lady wearing bright red lipstick thrust her shovel into the ground, stomped up to us, and announced to *Oum* Palla that they had only five more days until the monks returned. Then she pointed to the building with the unfinished yellow and orange paint job, the hole in the ground that hadn't been dealt with, and the picnic tables that were lined up in an area that was supposed to be a flower garden. She wore the most serious-looking face I'd ever seen.

Oum Palla touched her on the arm. "Don't worry, *Bang*, we'll get everything done in time."

"For real, we'll get that pond done, too," Chet added. Then he got the idea that we could float paper lanterns in the water—"You know, send *Oum* Naree down the river," he explained—but *Oum* Palla called him stupid and told him that what he was referring to was a *Japon* tradition.

Oum Palla said to the lady, "He's twenty. But he knows nothing. A bachelor. Going to college. And I don't know when he'll ever get done."

Nahrin, Mom, and the lady laughed. Chet shrugged and said that he had to help supervise the painters. I watched him walk away from us, not understanding why he wasn't pissed off.

To Mom the lady said, "You're *Bang* Naree's daughter?"

Mom *chumreap suor*-ed her and answered, "Yes," smiling warmly.

The lady bunched up her lips. "So sad. Your mother led such a sad life. And now she's *slab heiy*."

The smile on Mom's face vanished.

Nahrin gently told his mother that the inside of the

temple was in great need of organization, and we said good-bye to the lady.

We took off our shoes at the entrance of the temple, and *Oum* Palla led me to a large open room where there were many people.

We passed a built-in bookcase containing varied sizes of framed pictures of people who, I thought, had died. I searched for my father, but he was not there. Most of them were old people, some ladies whose smiles revealed no teeth. Next to most of the pictures were urns.

The four of us excused ourselves as we made our way through women sewing pillowcases to the other end of the room. As they got on their knees in front of a life-size ceramic reclining Buddha, whose smile was as lovely as Sleeping Beauty's, I stared at him. I had never seen a sculpture of him before. There was no temple in Scottsville, and Grandma had only two small framed pictures that she sat beside her candles. Above him, hanging from the ceiling, was a canopy, and around the edges hung green, orange, and yellow tassels. Wooden steps leading up to him were filled with empty flower vases, and jars and cups of candles and burnt incense sticks.

Oum Palla lit each of us three incense sticks. She spoke under her breath, and I could make out her saying "watch over us" and "help us to be rich." We bowed three times and placed our burning incense sticks in a jar filled with uncooked rice. The room was beginning to smell like smoke and jasmine.

A circle of old, frail women with shaved heads sat in one corner counting candles and arranging them by size.

Then, to my amazement, one of them spat red juice into a jar. I pointed my finger at her, and Nahrin gently pushed it down. After what I had learned about him and my dad, I understood that Nahrin was like me: we have no say in what my mother does or does not do.

"It's okay. It's betel juice," he said.

"What's betel juice?" I asked.

"Betel is a type of nut. It's red. They chew on it."

"It's nasty."

"Grace," Mom said, and I shut up.

Two of the old ladies recognized my mother and waved their hands at her. We walked over to them, and she *chum-reap suor*-ed them.

"Oh, Chandra, I am so sad about your mother," one of them said in a deep voice. Her ears were big and long.

My mother politely nodded at all of the old women, and after several seconds she excused us, telling them that we had something to do.

"Okay," Big-Eared Lady said kindly to her. "But come back and talk to me. I haven't seen you in so long."

Mom awkwardly smiled at her and promised that she would.

Maly got up off the floor and waved wildly at us. That day, like my mother and me, she wore her hair up in a ponytail. Mom groaned behind me.

We joined Maly, who was sitting with her fiancé, David. Until that day I had never seen a David like him. I had always thought all Davids were white. David in the Bible, Michelangelo's David, and David in my class. This

David was Cambodian. But this David was also half Chinese, I would later find out. He was very light-skinned, almost the color of an egg, with a clean haircut. He was wearing a pink long-sleeve Polo shirt with the sleeves rolled up to his forearms, and dangling around his left wrist was a serious gold bracelet. All I could think as I stared at him was that Maly got herself a rich man.

David shook our hands.

Around Maly were colorful beads, like the ones hanging from the canopy. She explained that she was decorating pillows. *Oum* Palla told Mom and me to sit down and help her. I eagerly did so but noticed that my mother was scanning the room for something else to assist with.

"I'm so happy to see you, Chandra," Maly said.

"Well, I'm happy to see you, too," Mom said. Finally she sat between me and Nahrin.

"It's been so long."

"Yes, it has."

Mom said I couldn't use a needle, and instructed me to give her the colored droplets and she would sew them. I divided a new bag of beads into cool colors of green and blue.

Maly winked at me and asked her fiancé, "Isn't she the cutest?" David was discussing with Nahrin the most profitable way to invest donations from the parishioners, and he quickly told her that she was right, and I beamed.

My mother seemed unfazed.

Maly put down her pillowcase. "Do you remember, Chandra, how *Bang* Nahrin got away with everything?"

149

She didn't wait for Mom to answer, but touched *Oum* Palla on the shoulder. "Why is that, *Oum*? Why is it that boys are treated so differently from girls?"

"How should I know?" *Oum* Palla asked. "I'm a girl myself."

Maly told *Oum* Palla that she could see the obvious, but that it didn't answer why boys got to do certain things that girls didn't.

"I agree," I said to her. Mom briefly glared at me.

"For instance, Grace," Maly said, "all my brothers and Nahrin and Chet went to all the football games they wanted to. They hung out until they were ready to come home. They even got a car. Your mom and me, we had to come straight home."

"So, *Bang* Maly, did you and my mom always go to the same school?"

"Yes and no. By the time I came to the U.S., your mom knew a little English already. We started the sixth grade together. And we went to ESOL classes together."

"What's that?"

"ESOL? It's a class for non-Americans. For people like us. Who need to learn English."

"Oh," I said.

"Remember, Chandra, we baked sugar cookies all the time?"

Mom smiled stiffly at Maly.

I asked, "What else did you do?"

Maly had to think about my question. Then she whispered to me, "The boys were so bad, Grace."

"Yeah? How?"

Nahrin looked at us. "What?" he asked defensively.

"You act all innocent now," Maly said to him. "But I remember what you and those boys did. You made fun of us all the time."

"Not all of you."

"Well. It doesn't matter. It was awful how you guys tormented that Thai girl."

"What did they do?" I asked.

"Well, at that time, there weren't many Asians in our school," Maly said. "We were like mutes in class. But when we got to ESOL class, it was like we were dogs freed from our crates. We talked mostly in our language, which frustrated our ESOL teacher so much. There were six of us. Four Cambodians, one Thai girl, and a Vietnamese guy. The Thai girl, well, she was a bit overweight."

"And the guys made fun of her size," I suggested. "Oh, no."

"Yep. They were trying to get her to say the word 'pig' in Cambodian. And then they got the Vietnamese boy to teach us the word 'pig' in his language. It was pretty awful."

"Yeah," I agreed.

"Younger days," Nahrin said sheepishly. "I now know better."

"You should have known then!" I said. "She's probably a model or something now."

Maly hugged me sideways.

She let go of me, and I asked, "How about my—" I cut off my question as soon as I saw Mom's wary eyes.

"What?" Maly asked.

"Nothing," I answered quickly, figuring that I would

soon learn anyway if my father had gotten away with as many things as Nahrin and Chet, or if he even liked football games.

"How is Atlanta, Chandra?" Maly asked Mom.

"We live in Pennsylvania," she said.

"Oh," Maly said. "Well, it was nice of your mom to make so many moves with you, huh?"

My mother tightly grinned, her lips barely noticeable. "Yes, she was a nice, unselfish woman." I wasn't sure if anyone else could, but I heard the anger in my mother's voice. "Too bad your mom can't go with you . . . after the wedding, Maly. I heard you will be moving to Seattle without her. Are you nervous about being on your own, away from her? In a new town with new people? Do you think you'll be okay without her telling you what to do?"

I looked up to see the stunned expression on Maly's face. Nahrin and David must have heard my mother, too, for they had stopped talking. Now they were studying the beads.

"Of course she will be," *Oum* Palla said gently to Mom. "She's a big girl." She had spoken in a voice that told you she was defending Maly, but it was my mother whom she loved more.

A few minutes later Maly's mother came to our circle. *Oum* Palla patted the spot beside her. "Sit, sit," she ordered *Yeay* Mao.

Yeay Mao held on to her back with one hand and slowly squatted down with us. "Look at you, Chandra. You're old ripe."

Mom politely smiled and *chumreap suor*-ed her.

"Maly, we mother and daughter are lucky, huh? Chandra came right in time. Aren't we lucky that her daughter will be in your wedding?" I was a little confused by her enthusiasm.

Maly answered, *"Chas, chas."*

I gulped and noticed that *Oum* Palla glanced up from her pillow. Earlier that afternoon I had told her of Mom's decision on the bridesmaid situation.

"About that," Mom said to Maly. "We have so much to do for the funeral. I'm afraid that Grace will not be able to serve as one of your bridesmaids."

"What?" Maly asked. She looked at Nahrin and me for assistance, but I was too afraid to help her, and Nahrin kept his mouth shut, too.

Mom said to *Yeay* Mao, "We didn't come prepared. I don't want for us to make any mistakes in Maly's wedding."

"Don't say that, Chandra. I've already spoken to the wedding dresser about measuring your daughter," *Yeay* Mao said.

Mom breathed deeply; she was getting into her teacher mode. She often did that when she talked to her students' parents on the phone, when she was trying not to tell them how rude and ignorant their kids were. "I'm sorry, but it's not a good idea."

Yeay Mao opened her mouth, but no sound came out of it. Maly nervously rolled some beads on her rosy palm. And Nahrin, David, and I kept quiet.

"Chandra," *Oum* Palla sternly said. "Your *oum* is asking for your help. Help her. What are you going to gain or lose from this?"

Mom did not answer. It wasn't one of those questions that was expected to be answered. It was just understood: I would be in the wedding.

The sun was directly on us, and I felt it penetrating my scalp as Mom and I stood outside. Droplets of sweat were starting to roll down the sides of my mother's face. I looked out across the backyard of the temple, at a guy in cutoffs finishing mowing the lawn. When he was done, Chet and a couple of other men pulled out the picnic benches and aligned them side by side.

I wanted to remind Chet what he had promised to help me with, and I was considering walking up to him, when three young girls swarmed him like bees. They were giggling, and he was, too. One of them pretended to kick him on the shin. When he pointed at me, they turned to me. And I couldn't believe what I saw at first. As I felt the heat of embarrassment surfacing my face, I squinted to make sure I was seeing correctly. And when I realized that I was, that the three girls were the same ones I'd seen at the mall, I quickly turned away.

Mom tugged me on the shoulder and ordered, "Pay attention."

A man wearing a long scarf wrapped around his head said that we could help with painting the steps to the back porch. "Prime first," he instructed, and pointed to the can and paintbrushes.

After he left, I said to Mom, "I'm sorry that I'll be in *Bang* Maly's wedding."

She waved her hand to tell me not to worry about it, and grabbed one of the brushes. "Don't get me wrong, Grace," my mother said. "I don't dislike Maly. She's a fine person, I'm sure. It's just that things change. Even if we don't want them to. We live our lives for years and think things are going the way they're supposed to. We get used to certain beliefs. But then one morning we wake up and we know. We know that what we believed was a fake. Everything we once thought was true never was."

I knew that Mom's and Maly's lives had verged onto two different roads. Mom had gotten knocked up when she was only eighteen years old. Maly . . . she was probably a thirty-three-year-old virgin. Even though Mom may have regretted that one night with my father, I believed that many people would have wanted her life. So there had to be more to make my mother question her beliefs. "What is not true?"

"Nothing." Mom dipped a large brush in the can and began to stroke it back and forth on the top step, some of the white primer splattering onto the new grass. "I'll be glad when this is over."

"The painting?" I asked. "I'm sure we can find something else to do, if you want."

"No, not the painting. I'm talking about—" She pointed to the people around us. "I'm talking about this."

I didn't understand her change of mood. Just this afternoon, after she'd gotten back from shopping with Nahrin, she'd mentioned how much she wanted all of St. Pete to attend Grandma's funeral.

"Yeah, but when we go back home, you're not going to see them again," I said. "Aren't you going to miss them?" I was thinking about *Oum* Palla, Nahrin, and Chet, who was now laying plastic in the pond.

"I'm not talking about the people. I'm talking about their beliefs, Grace. Some of these people, like that woman earlier, believed that your grandmother's life was so sad and that it was destined for doom. And your grandma believed them." Mom snorted. "But what gets me is that they have all the evidence to prove themselves right. 'I mean, my gosh, Naree's daughter got pregnant and wasn't married and then Naree died so young.' Hell, what better validation is there for them? It's like they got rewarded for believing that your grandmother had such a sad and pathetic life."

I thought about all that my grandmother had gone through. The humiliation. The pain. No wonder she had been so disillusioned and needed my mother so much. I felt a shiver going up my right arm. "She did have a sad life."

"No, she didn't," Mom said firmly. "She had a daughter who cared about her. And a grandchild who loved her. She had sad moments, but not a sad life."

I didn't understand the difference. "It's not these people's fault for feeling sorry for her. It's Grandma's dad. If he hadn't humiliated her, then . . ."

"Then what?" Mom peered into me. I took a deep swallow, hoping no one nearby would hear her. "If he hadn't pulled down her sarong on that damn night, then what would have happened? Would your grandma have had a better life? A different life? Would the sun have shone more brightly on her than on someone else?"

Would it? Maybe. Her life was horrible. Maybe she would have been luckier and led a life with less scars if her father had been kinder. I didn't know what to say.

"Grace, I'm so tired of that backward story," Mom said. "You and other people who think your great-grandfather doomed your grandmother's future are giving him more credit than he deserves. A man does not make a woman. Do you understand that? You can't allow anything to hold you back. This is what I've been trying to tell you. Break away from your past and live."

That was easy for my mother to say. She had a choice to do whatever she wanted with her past. I was still trying to collect mine.

10

The next morning, I found Chet in the backyard watering his mother's fruit trees. Nahrin had already left for work, and I wanted to catch Chet before he went to his English class. Even though it was still early, several lawn mowers were already running in the neighborhood, and somewhere, someone was drilling a hole in the street. "Good morning," I said.

"Well, here comes the bridesmaid." Chet turned the hose on the bed of mints and basil. The dark green leaves fluttered beneath the water, and once in a while I caught a whiff of their sweet, fresh scent. Chet shot the water at my feet, and I dodged it.

I moved to stand under the longan tree, letting the tips of its leaves tickle my head. "So, how's the investigation going?" The day before, when we had gotten home, he had told me that one of the three girls he had spoken to at temple had given him a good lead on my father. The girl had told him that she had heard her parents talk about a young man who had drowned. Chet also said that the girls had asked him about me, wanting to know if I was his girl-friend; he had told all three of them I was his little cousin.

"Sorry, kid. It was a bad lead. The guy that she was talking about isn't who we're looking for. That guy was older than your dad."

"Really? Are you *sure* sure?"

"Yeah. Sorry."

"But did you at least tell her to talk to her parents some more?"

Chet began to spray the pepper plants. "Grace, we have to do this very carefully. I'll help you. Promise. But we have to think about your mom, too."

"Everyone's thinking about her," I said.

Chet scrunched up his face at me. "Huh?"

"She does whatever she wants, and no one asks ques-tions."

Chet returned to the plants, and I watched the water turning the soil a rich black color, and tried to understand this unconditional love that *Oum* Palla and her sons had for my mother. I wondered if they knew that I loved her more, even though I was bad-mouthing her.

Later I said, "What about your brother? Didn't he wonder where she'd gone, after she left this place?" He shrugged. "She already told me how serious their relation-ship was." When he still didn't respond, I added, "I would just like to know, that's all."

With his eyes unwavering from the plants, he finally

said, "After she and your grandma left St. Pete, Nahrin spent almost a year living in Georgia looking for your mom."

"Then?" I asked.

"Then he stopped."

"Why?" If they had had the connection that I thought they had, I pictured Nahrin lying in bed sleepless, wondering about Mom's well-being. "Wasn't he afraid that she had died or something?"

Chet looked at me. "You have a good point. I don't know why none of us thought that. We all just thought your mom and grandma were okay. That they wanted things this way." He shrugged again.

I could see what he meant. Other than when she cried after Grandma had died, I'd never seen my mother being not okay. She did everything for a reason and with a purpose. "Did your brother have other girlfriends? My mom didn't."

"Nahrin? Yeah. A couple. But nothing serious. It'd always been your mom, even when he stopped talking about her."

I couldn't imagine being in someone's mind for fourteen years. I wondered if Nahrin had known that Mom was pregnant when she and Grandma ran, that Mom had had sex with another guy, a guy that she wasn't even in love with, just because she wanted to rebel. I wondered, too, why Mom hadn't just done it with Nahrin to begin with. Things would have turned out much easier. But whether Nahrin had known then about my mother's big mistake, he knew now, and it didn't seem to matter to him. I could see it in his eyes when he looked at me. I felt sad for my dad then, certain that any special connection he had had with that special someone had ended too soon.

I followed Chet to the side of the house, and he turned off the spigot, then put a hand on the door.

"I have a plan," he said. "I'll go to the high schools and look at their yearbooks. If your dad went to school here, he should be in one of the yearbooks, and then I'll get a good idea of the Cambodian guys he went to school with. And then we can start investigating like you said, like Magnum, okay?"

I jumped up and down. "Oh my God! That's brilliant! You're brilliant!" I could have reached out and kissed him. "And I can help you. We'll go together."

Chet shook his head. "No, no. We don't want your mom or my mom to ask questions."

I snapped my fingers at him. "That's true. We don't want them to suspect anything. You are a true genius."

"Well, once in a while," he said.

I started to open the door when Chet told me to wait. "Oh, one more thing."

"Yeah?" I asked.

"Those girls who asked if you were my girlfriend were positive that they'd seen you somewhere." And he winked at me.

Maly had called very early on that Monday morning and asked if we could help with her wedding reception. David, with a warm smile, opened the door for *Oum* Palla, Mom, and me.

As we took off our shoes, Maly came down the stairs and apologized. She and her mother had been debating whether the apricot-colored gown was appropriate for *Yeay* Mao to wear at the wedding reception. "You don't know how tough it is to plan a wedding, Chandra," *Yeay* Mao said.

"No, I don't," Mom said.

Maly poured pretzels into a large bowl and took it with her to a room in the back of the house. We waved good-bye to David, who sat at the dining table with his laptop, and we followed Maly. *Yeay* Mao and *Oum* Palla were talking about a kid who had gotten caught breaking into someone's house. "*Bang,* when something like that happens, where do the parents hide their faces?" *Yeay* Mao asked.

Oum Palla said that she didn't know. She was just grateful that her sons were grown.

Maly's exercise room had boxes and boxes of white tulle, glass vases, candles, greenery, pink and red silk flowers, and twig wreaths just waiting to be adorned. "Oh my God," I said.

"Are you excited, Grace? I've been collecting these things for the past six months. Can you believe it? As much as it is fun to look at everything, though, I'll be glad once they're out of here and I can pull out my treadmill."

"But aren't you moving?" Mom reminded her.

"Yeah. I am," Maly said forlornly.

"Who's going to do the decoration at the hall for you?" I asked.

"Oh, the wedding dresser's nieces." She put her hand

on my shoulder. "And you know the wedding dresser is going over to *Oum* Palla's to measure you tonight, right?"

I nodded calmly. Secretly, though, I couldn't wait to see what I would be wearing. Something inside of me told me that my dad's family would be at the wedding. I would stand out that day. Surely they would see me and know that I belonged to them.

"Pink and red are your colors?" Mom asked.

"White and pink, actually. But David's mom insisted that we have some red. So we are." Maly shrugged, and I truly admired her for giving in so easily to a poor color combination. I was sure that I would have gone down fighting.

Maly had already laid out what we were supposed to do. *Oum* Palla and *Yeay* Mao hadn't stopped for air as they continued to discuss the hardships of raising perfect children. They simply glided down onto the floor, sitting around the neat piles of small silk flowers, green leaves, green floral tape, ribbons, pins, and scissors.

"I'm so grateful you can help. We've started making these corsages. But as you can see, we're not done. I've been so busy at the dental office and David's parents are coming in two days, and I don't want them to know that they're not finished," Maly said to us. I learned that the only other time she had seen her in-laws was six months earlier, when they came down for the engagement ceremony.

I sat beside *Oum* Palla. "It's no problem at all."

"Your daughter's truly unbelievable," Maly said to Mom, who seemed to have tuned out.

"Okay, we pin these tiny corsages on women guests at the reception," Maly told me. "Take a flower, a leaf, and tape them together at the stem with the green tape. And stick a pin through it. Just like this. You see, it's easy." Once Maly was done with the example, she held it up for all of us to see, and asked her mother if what she had done was correct.

"Yes, yes, *Coan,*" *Yeay* Mao replied.

"How many do we have to make?" I asked.

"We invited three hundred guests. But we need to make only about a hundred more."

"Three hundred people!" I exclaimed. "That's a lot of people." Mom didn't seem impressed, though. She had already started on the flowers. "All of them in this house?"

Maly giggled and explained, "No, not everyone comes to the ceremony. Only close friends and family. But everyone will go to the reception."

Oum Palla and *Yeay* Mao had finally finished their discussion of the young thief, and from what I gathered, *Yeay* Mao thought that the best place for parents to hide their faces was in a different town. She looked across at Mom. "So, how are you, Chandra?"

"Fine, thank you," my mother answered.

"Was your mom sick for long? I didn't know. Otherwise, I would have called her. To think that we have come this far together and to be separated like we were. Not a single phone call."

Mom politely said, "No, she wasn't sick for very long."

"And her burn scar. Did she ever get that fixed? I can't believe—"

"No," Mom interrupted her. "My mother was fine with it." She sounded just like Grandma had. A couple of times Mom mentioned to Grandma that her burn could be taken care of with plastic surgery, but all that my grand-mother would say was, "No, I am fine with it."

We were all so quiet that I heard David turn on the TV in the other room.

Yeay Mao abruptly switched her attention to *Oum* Palla. "David's mom just told me about a girl in Seattle. Did I tell you?"

"What girl?" *Oum* Palla asked.

"Are you sure I didn't tell you already?"

"How do I know? I don't even know what girl you're talking about," *Oum* Palla reasoned.

"Listen, then. She got married to an *Americ,* went to church, and became *Kristen* like her husband. So sad. When her mother died, she had the church do the funeral. Mother. No food, no candles. No one could *tweu bouhn.* Nothing proper. Can you believe that?"

"What happened?" *Oum* Palla asked.

"The mother's spirit didn't go anywhere. It stayed here. At night she visited her daughter, pleading that she was so hungry. 'So hungry, so hungry.'"

"How do you know?"

"What?" *Yeay* Mao asked, offended. "What? You don't believe me? If you want to know, David's mom told me. The daughter went to her one day, crying. Saying that her mother won't leave her alone. 'What should I do?' the girl asked. Well, David's mom is very educated. She told the girl, 'Your mother's not *Kristen* and believe in Jesus like you and your husband. Don't worry about making your husband upset. If you don't want your mother to come and visit you at night anymore, give her a proper Cambodian ceremony.' The girl did. And the mother stopped coming. It was like she was full and ready to go wherever she needed to go. You understand?"

Oum Palla grunted that she did understand. Then she added proudly, "Naree isn't visiting Chandra at night. Chandra is giving her mother a Cambodian funeral because she knows it's the right thing to do. Daughters are responsible like that. I don't know if I can depend on my sons. I don't even know what to do with them."

"Find them good wives," *Yeay* Mao answered.

"Huh! It's not that easy, *Yeay* Mao. It's not like when we were kids. Most kids these days find their own husbands and wives. You can't choose for them. If you try, they tell you that they're smart enough to choose for themselves."

"That's true, but you got to tell them who they are. Tell them what's right and wrong. You have to be the mother. And if they love you, then they will listen to what you say and do what you say. Look at my daughter. Do you know how many men were interested in her?"

"*Mak*," Maly squealed. She pointed her scissors at the door, at David, who must have been at least one hundred feet away from us.

Yeay Mao didn't seem to hear her daughter. "Five men. From good families. All of their parents came and talked to me and her father properly. And like David, all of them are grandchild Chinese." She meant they were part Chinese.

166

"Five men wanted to marry you?" I asked Maly. She gently placed a finger to her lips. "Five men wanted to marry you?" I whispered. She bashfully nodded. "You had five boyfriends at the same time?"

Maly shook her head. "Oh, no."

This amazed me even more. "They weren't your boyfriends, and they wanted to marry you? For real?"

Maly proudly nodded, but I was still confused. I knew that I was learning a lot about Cambodians. But the idea of not having to have a boyfriend but still getting to have a husband made me care less that boys and girls were treated differently. In the end, we would get the same thing.

"So how did you decide on *Bang* David?" I asked.

She opened her mouth, but Mom was too fast for her. "You didn't choose, did you, Maly? I'm sure you left that tough job up to your mom, right?"

Thankfully, *Oum* Palla and *Yeay* Mao were counting the corsages and hadn't seemed to hear the bitterness in my mother's voice.

"My parents and I did," Maly said.

"Of course, you did," Mom added.

Maly's eyes and lips were bunched up in frustration, but my mother refused to acknowledge her as she continued to do what we'd been asked to accomplish. Of all of us, she'd completed the most corsages; there was already a high pile in front of her.

"How did *Bang* David find out about *Bang* Maly?" I asked *Yeay* Mao.

"Word of mouth," she answered casually, and with

great pride. "When David turned thirty-five last year, his mother had her sisters and cousins and everyone else she knew search around for a young woman who might be a good match for him. When David's mom heard that Maly was grandchild Chinese, too, that she was a dentist, and had had no boyfriends, she knew Maly would be perfect for David." Then she said to *Oum* Palla. "And David is good, too. So many girls like him."

"That is so good," *Oum* Palla agreed.

I took a break and moved the bowl of pretzels in front of me.

Maly caught me watching her. "So, what's your favorite subject in school?"

I hated that question. It was as though one of the seven subject areas had to be more attractive than the others. Couldn't all subject matters suck equally? "I don't have one. You know, I'm just going through the motions. Waiting for the day I can get out of school," I said.

Maly put down the leaf she'd been twirling and hit her thigh as she laughed at me. I loved it that she found me funny. "Okay, then. What do you want to be when you're older?"

"A teacher."

"Like your mom, huh? I remember that she wanted to be a teacher forever. Even when we were in middle school, she used to line up her stuffed animals on her bed, and she would talk to them like they were her students. Some nights, when I slept over, she would let me be the substitute teacher."

"Really? Was she a good teacher?"

Maly laughed again, but Mom still had her head in the flowers. "Oh, she was very good. She took the attendance, wrote up the troublemakers."

"No, she did not!" I screamed.

Mom told me to quiet down, and Maly playfully frowned at her.

"What was she like in school?" I asked. "I bet you guys were really popular."

Maly asked me to hand her the scissors. "Your mom was very studious. Very quiet."

"Oh, no. Was she a loner?"

"In a way, we were all loners because we didn't speak much English. The teachers loved your mom, though. I remember one time. I think we were in the eighth grade. We'd all gone to the book fair, and your mom bought a book. Well, she left it under her desk when she went to the bathroom. And when she came back, her book was gone. Someone had stolen it. So she told the teacher. Well, the teacher was so angry that one of her students would steal, especially from one of us Cambodians—we were all so poor. So she made everyone—except your mom—write a one-page report on why honesty was important in our society."

"Oh my God. That is so embarrassing. I bet the kids hated her after that day."

"I thought they would, too. But they weren't any meaner to her than usual."

"Did she ever find her book?"

"Your mom had an idea as to who stole it. She asked the kid about it, but he denied stealing it. Even made fun of her for asking him."

"What did he do?"

"Ah, he made fun of how she spoke. Kept saying to her, 'What? What—did—you—say?' Your mom said that if he would show her the inside of the cover, she'd show him her name. But he refused to. So at lunch, she talked me into getting extra packets of ketchup. We waited for the moment he and his friends were in the lunch line. And when they were, we walked over to their table and opened the book, found her name in the corner, and smeared the inside cover and several other pages with ketchup."

"No, she did not! That's awful. Mom, I wouldn't have wanted to mess with you."

"It was a long time ago," my mother said. "And, Maly, I've been meaning to ask, when did you get your mole?"

"What are you talking about?" Maly asked.

Mom's eyes remained steady on the flower stem she was working on. "The mole above your lips. You never had it before. And your eyebrows. When did you shave off the real ones and get those painted on?"

Maly blushed, and *Oum* Palla frowned. Not understanding the language well, *Yeay* Mao had no clue what was going on and did not say anything to defend her daughter.

"Oh, Chandra," *Oum* Palla said casually. "Tattooed makeup is very popular with young people. It's convenient, too. Right, Maly?"

Although I hoped that Mom would not think that I was betraying her, I said to Maly, "And it looks good, too."

Maly smiled weakly at us and got up to rearrange the folded tulle.

The phone rang, and *Yeay* Mao answered it. "H'lo, h'lo." She shook her head at us furiously and handed the phone to her daughter. *"Americ."*

As Maly spoked into the phone, *Yeay* Mao told her that if it was a credit card company, to let her know. She had canceled all of credit lines, but now she wanted one again. "It's good to build credit," she said to *Oum* Palla. "In case you want to open a business or something."

"Yes, she is my mother," Maly said. She covered the phone and said to her mom in Cambodian, "It's Discover. Did Dad fill out an application for you?" *Yeay* Mao answered a positive, and Maly said to the caller, "Yes, she sent in an application." We were all silent as we listened to Maly and Discover talk. Seconds later she covered the phone again and asked her mom, "You've been approved for a credit line of ten thousand dollars. Do you want to do a balance transfer?" *Yeay* Mao didn't understand "balance transfer." Maly explained that if she had a loan or other credit cards, she could move the balance over to Discover and not pay interest on it for the next year. Her mother got incredulous. She had not borrowed money from anyone, and she hadn't even used a credit card in the past five years. She had used only cash. Then she asked if *Oum* Palla knew what she was talking about. Maly told Discover that her mother was not interested in balance transfers at this time. She thanked Discover for calling and hung up.

"Now what?" *Yeay* Mao asked Maly.

"They said you will get your card in about two weeks."

"Good. Good," *Yeay* Mao said, and added to *Oum* Palla, "*Americ* is so easy." She grinned so wide that you'd think her life was perfect.

But, of course, I knew her life wasn't perfect. Like Grandma, *Yeay* Mao had to rely on her daughter to understand English. And because of that, I knew, *Americ* was not easy. Not for people like her. But I also wondered why, like Grandma, she didn't go to school to learn English, and make her life and her daughter's life much easier.

Maly and the wedding dresser came to the house before dinner, and as soon as Maly stepped inside she whined. "It's raining. What am I going to do, *Oum*? It can't rain on Saturday. Everything will be ruined." *Oum* Palla told her that it was only Monday, and Saturday was five days away.

Mom was also worried about the weather; she had told me that she was certain the rain would prevent people from attending Grandma's funeral.

Mom and I sat with Maly and the wedding dresser in the living room. Ever since the visit to the temple yesterday, my mother had been quiet, but now she was almost silent, with hands folded in her lap. This time, though, she seemed like a nervous student rather than a teacher.

Oum Palla brought jasmine tea from the kitchen, and she asked if I would pour some for everyone. I got on my knees and tried to do it without spilling any. The teapot handle was hot, but I didn't want to make a fuss by asking for a holder. So I did my best and ended up filling each cup only halfway. As I handed *Meing* Huor, the wedding dresser, her teacup, she asked Maly in Cambodian, "Is this the child?"

Maly said that I was.

Meing Huor studied me, and I couldn't decide if she was smiling, trying to hold back a frown, or constipated. "How old are you?" she asked.

"Fourteen, *Meing,*" I answered, calling her Aunt.

"That's her mother," Maly said, pointing to my mother.

Meing Huor started to bellow in the loudest laugh I'd ever heard from a woman's body. "Oh, it is you, Chandra! Why are you sitting there acting like you don't know me?"

Tears started to show in Mom's eyes, and I did not know why. And I would not know until much later, that those tears on my mother's cheeks were beyond joy. I would not know until later when Mom told me that *Meing* Huor had been a neighbor of hers, whom she considered a big sister, who had promised to dress her up and make her the prettiest bride when the day came. Whom Mom hadn't said good-bye to when she and Grandma left St. Pete.

"I was waiting to see if you would recognize me, *Bang,*" she said.

"Oh, I missed you so much," *Meing* Huor said. She placed her teacup gently on the coffee table, got up from the sofa, and walked to kiss Mom on the face. "I can't believe you never called me."

Mom didn't say anything, but we all knew that she couldn't believe it, either.

Meing Huor's suitcase was standing beside the dining table, and from the sofa I watched as she opened the luggage, revealing a high pile of shimmering fabric. As beautiful as it was, I wondered where the real dresses were, the ones I had seen in magazines. Weren't they supposed to be hanging on fancy hangers in large plastic bags?

"Come here," *Meing* Huor ordered me.

Nervously I put down my teacup and walked toward the wedding dresser. She gently removed each piece of fabric from the suitcase and lined them up on the table. The fabrics were ones that I was not used to wearing. Some were pure silk, *Oum* Palla would tell me later. Some were lace. *Meing* Huor explained to me that I would wear five different outfits, one on Friday night, three during Saturday's long ceremony, and another one at the reception on Saturday evening.

"Five outfits!" I screamed.

Everyone laughed, even my mother.

Meing Huor proudly told *Oum* Palla and Maly that everything she had was new. She had just brought it back from Cambodia two months earlier. "Of all the wedding dressers in Florida, Georgia, and Virginia, only I have new, modern dresses," she said. She also informed us that she had just received a phone call from a family in Jacksonville who wanted her as their wedding dresser. "That is such an important family. Their daughter is a doctor. A surgeon!"

Oum Palla told *Meing* Huor that she was very popular.

I watched Mom from the corner of my eye. She was holding the teacup still. As genuine as her smile was, I was sorry that I had opened my big mouth and agreed to be in Maly's wedding when I first met her. I'd never seen Mom flip pages of bridal magazines. She's never had a longing look on her face when we drove by bridal shops. Not having a wedding never seemed to have been a big issue for Mom, even though it had been to Grandma. It seemed that for Mom, it was one of those things that just wasn't. But now I could see how my mother might have wanted things differently. Earlier that day, *Yeay* Mao had spoken so proudly of her daughter. Did Mom feel that Grandma would have been more proud of her if she'd had a wedding? I wondered if she would change her mind about Nahrin's proposal.

"And I will be the first to wear what you have, right, *Bang*?" Maly asked *Meing* Huor.

"Of course, I knew you would have a big wedding, so I wanted to be sure to have all brand-new things. You'll be the first to rent my dresses."

"Doesn't *Bang* Maly buy the dresses?" I asked.

Meing Huor told me no and said to Mom, "Chandra, you don't teach your kid anything?"

My chin dropped, but my mother just grinned, her eyes half closed, as though she were daydreaming.

"My mom is a math teacher," I said. And the women in the room laughed again.

Meing Huor pinched my cheek. "It's okay. Come live with me awhile, and I'll teach you everything, *Khmuy*." Niece.

From the corner of my eye, I saw Mom smile so hugely that I thought she would burst from happiness, and I was no longer offended.

Meing Huor explained to me that each outfit was very

expensive, about five hundred dollars a set, and the average bride, on top of her white American gown, would wear anywhere from five to seven of them.

"*Bang* Huor. American kid. What does she know?" *Oum* Palla asked her.

Meing Huor asked if I wanted to try on the dresses there, in front of everyone, or in a bedroom.

"Here." I pulled off my shirt and stepped out of my clean shorts, standing in my bra and a brand-new Hanes Her Way.

"American kids aren't embarrassed at all," she said.

"Why should she be?" *Oum* Palla asked in a friendly tone. "We're all girls here."

Meing Huor touched the first outfit, which was pink. She picked up the top material and unfolded it. The pink lacy fabric was just a long rectangle. She grabbed a couple of safety pins from her suitcase and held them between her lips as she began to wrap one end of the material around my chest. Her fingertips were cold while she secured the fabric with a pin under my armpit, and the excess material she flung across and over my right shoulder, then pinned down somewhere on my back. She picked up another piece of fabric that was also pink, and silk like *Yeay* Mao's dress. She held it open with both hands so that it looked like a hula hoop, and told me to step inside. Once I was in it, she stood up with the material, and I felt as though I'd just stepped into a pillowcase with two ends open. The thick silk was not soft, and rustled when *Meing* Huor pulled the extra material to the front and folded it into multiple pleats, which she held in place with a fancy silver belt around my waist. "This is *phamourng*," she said, tugging on the skirt.

"You look beautiful," Maly exclaimed. From the brilliance in everyone's eyes, I thought that I must have been.

"In Cambodia, all brides—poor or rich—look the same. They all look like children of kings and queens," *Oum* Palla said.

"Not true," *Meing* Huor challenged. "Not around Pol Pot. Huh, my sisters all got married in a rush. They didn't wear nice things like this or do everything they were supposed to in the wedding. Some of them were lucky if they could just go to temple and have the monks splash holy water on them. And during Pol Pot, huh, just a couple of incense sticks and candles. And that was all."

"Well, that was during Pol Pot. Everything then was done just to get it done."

As *Oum* Palla and *Meing* Huor continued to compare weddings during peacetime and wartime, I excused myself and broke away for the bathroom.

Standing in front of the mirror, I saw that I was a step closer to looking like my mother. I saw myself in her dance pictures, her hair all made up, her body bejeweled like a true princess. Until then I had never worn anything Cambodian, and I was amazed that it felt as though every inch of my body had been measured for it. I twirled in a circle and strutted out my shoulders and butt, the pink of the silk *phamourng* shimmering and changing color slightly— soft pink, medium pink, bruised pink—all the while.

When I heard Chet's voice, I decided to catwalk to the living room.

"Whoa," he said when he saw me. His hair was wet, and he was rubbing rainwater off his arms.

"What do you think, *Bang* Chet?" I asked while doing my sexiest walk to him.

Chet studied me, and patted me on the head as he said, "Not too bad, kid. But you might want to tuck in your bra straps."

I slapped his hand off my head, and *Oum* Palla exclaimed that he was the rudest kid she had ever known.

11

We were watching the Weather Channel when Nahrin got home from work that Tuesday evening. Actually, we had been watching it for the past four hours. Neither *Oum* Palla nor Mom could break away from the TV as soon as Chief Weather Expert Donaldson mentioned the prospect of a hurricane forming out in the Keys.

"Another hurricane? Again?" *Oum* Palla had asked Mom, whose eyes were also glued to the television.

Then *Oum* Palla had asked me, and I had said, "I guess."

Mom had kept eyeing me nervously, until I told her that we would be back home before anything happened to St. Pete. Of course, I regretted saying it when I realized how inconsiderate I was of *Oum* Palla and her sons.

Now, before Nahrin could sit down, his mother

pointed to the weatherman. "Look at that. Again, son. And this time we might not be so lucky."

"Don't worry, *Mak*. St. Pete is usually safe," he said.

Chet walked out of his room and announced that he was hungry. He had just come home from taking a tough exam. He walked to the kitchen and asked if his girlfriend had called.

"I'm not your secretary," his mother said.

"And neither am I," I added.

Chet stretched out his arms at the dining table, laid the top half of his body on it, and moaned, "I want some pho."

"Should we go to the place on Sixty-second Street?" Mom asked.

"No, that one's been closed a long time," Nahrin said. "The wife ran off with the cook, and the husband became homeless."

"Really?" Mom was genuinely shocked. "But when I was around, the cook had only one leg."

Chet snorted, and when he began to speak, *Oum* Palla told him to shut up. "Son, you want to go to hell or something?"

At the hostess's station of the Vietnamese restaurant, we were greeted by a jolly Chinese Lucky Buddha holding sticks of incense. Chet told me that my wish would come true if I rubbed my hand on Buddha's stomach. I whispered that my wish would come true if he was working on finding my father's family; he said that he had everything under control.

"So," I said more loudly, "is this fat Buddha related

to the skinny Buddha?" The Buddha I'd seen at temple looked enlightened, as though the moon was shining behind his head, and serene, emanating peace, not laughing with his mouth open while little Chinese kids climbed on him.

"Fat Buddha is skinny Buddha well fed," Nahrin answered. Mom rolled her eyes at him.

At our table everyone knew what to order, except for me. I asked Mom for help, and she said that anything I ordered would be good. Chet suggested that I get number five, pho with well-cooked beef flanks.

When the food arrived, it seemed as though we'd all gotten the same noodle dish, but with variations of meats. Mom had ordered meatballs, Chet had ordered rare beef, and Nahrin got the special combination bowl, which included beef tripe and tendons. Without first asking me, Chet threw bean sprouts and cinnamon basil into my bowl and his, and handed me the hoisin sauce bottle and a pair of chopsticks.

"Uh," I said.

"What?" he asked.

"I don't know how to use these."

"Are you joking?"

"No, I'm not joking, okay?"

Nahrin called the waitress over and asked her to bring me a fork.

"How do you not know how to use chopsticks?" Chet went on.

"How do you not know when to stop talking?"

"Grace," Mom said.

I told Chet I was sorry. "But seriously, you think

because I'm Asian American I should know how to use chopsticks? I think you're more American than the American Americans." When he didn't respond, I asked, "How's your girlfriend, anyway?"

"I don't think she likes me anymore."

"It wasn't serious, man," Nahrin told him. Chet began to eat his rice noodles.

As we finished our food, the manager opened up the karaoke bar. Mom left to use the restroom. A group of patrons Mom's age and Chet's age had gathered at the tables in front of the microphone and television. They were dressed mostly in black and white and spoke Vietnamese. The girls were pretty, and the guys held cigarettes to their mouths in one hand and beer bottles in the other. The first girl, in a short black skirt and Mary Janes, went up on the low stage, and her friends cheered her on.

A while later Mom returned to the table. As she sat down Nahrin said, "A long time ago. A very long time ago." While she was in the bathroom, I had asked him about how he and she had fallen in love.

"It was so sweet," Chet cooed, "that it kept him up all night, like caffeine overload." Then he let out a cherub's sigh. His short second of cheeriness soon dissipated, his cheeks drooping like wet laundry and his eyes darting from one corner of the table to the next.

I felt for Chet—it was not fun to be the person in the relationship doing all the loving—but I couldn't afford to let his girlfriend crisis break Nahrin's concentration once he started the story. "Why don't you just call her, seeing as you miss her so much?"

"It's her turn to call, and if she doesn't, I don't care." Chet went back to staring at the table.

"Fine. But please don't interrupt the story, okay?"

Mom sat awkwardly beside Nahrin.

"Come on, *Bang* Nahrin, let's hear it. How did it all start?" I asked.

"Well, I remember that at the Thai camp," Nahrin began, "your mom was only seven years old. When all the rest of us kids played hooky, she was early for her English class. And when the teachers gave out candy, she didn't eat hers. She saved it for your grandma. She had always been a good girl. The only problem was that she liked me."

"I did not. You liked me first!" Mom exclaimed.

I asked Chet for confirmation. "In high school, you called the house all the time, *Bang* Chandra," he said.

Her eyes rounded in astonishment. "You were six years old! How would you remember if something like that even happened?"

"I remember," he insisted.

"If that was true, then I must have called to speak to your mom."

"At three o'clock in the afternoon? She was still at work. You knew that. I told you this every day when you called, but you always called at the same time. So then you would ask to speak to Nahrin." Chet changed his voice, attempting to sound like a little girl: " 'Ah . . . is *Bang* Nahrin home?' Like you didn't know he would be. Besides, if it wasn't true, you wouldn't be so upset now."

I giggled, and Mom's cheeks balled up into red apples, ripe enough to fall off the tree. Nahrin slapped his hand on the table, sending a chopstick flying across the room, where it landed on top of a purple silk rose in the large vase. "Thank you," he said to Chet.

When the waitress returned with the bill, Nahrin ordered *duran* milk shakes for all of us. He promised that they would be the best, better than a strawberry milk shake. As much as I liked him, I didn't believe him.

"Until your mom and I got married, we couldn't go anywhere together or be thought of as a couple," Nahrin said when the four of us were alone again.

"Cambodian ways are so out of order," I said.

"You're Cambodian," Chet said.

I pursed my lips at him. "Duh."

The waitress returned with four tall glasses of the *duran* milk shake. I held the barely yellow shake up to my nose and smelled it—a combination of overripe apples, pineapple, and flowers, if they were edible. It was sweet, like sugar and honeysuckle, but it was nothing close to a strawberry milk shake.

The singers across the room were packing up. One of the guys was counting his money, and threw it onto the table. A couple of the girls briefly held each other's hands before they all walked out.

Nahrin placed his hand on top of my mother's. The two shades of their brown skin blended beautifully, until she slowly inched her hand from underneath his weight. "I had feelings for your mother long before she had any feelings for me. But I didn't love her until much later," Nahrin said softly and longingly. Then he asked me, "Do you know what sympathy is?"

I felt the creases in my forehead deepening. "Yes. Sure. I guess."

"Well, that's what I felt for your mom."

That was it? Where was the romance? Where was the walking into walls because love put you in a daze? Sympathy! Sympathy was what you felt when you saw a dead deer on the road.

"You must feel sympathy for a person before you can love him or her. It's the most basic emotion that one human can have for another human being," Nahrin said. I nodded politely. "When your mom was a sophomore, she joined the math club at school."

Mom picked up her purse. "Let's go."

No one listened, and Nahrin placed his hand on her back. "Okay. There were math competitions between the schools, but until your mom joined the team, our school couldn't even compete because we sucked. Your mom was so good that we started competing, and we were winning. The team made her captain. Because of her, our school became division champions. It was unbelievable. Then we were regional champions. And for the first time in our school history, we were going for the state championship. She was even on the six o'clock news. And the newspaper did a whole page on her. Your mom and her teammates studied and practiced for weeks. They were supposed to travel to Gainesville for the state competition. But a week before the overnight trip, your grandma got into a car accident, and she broke her arm."

I sat back in my chair. "Wow."

"Your grandma was so scared that she didn't let your

mom leave her side. We all thought that once she left the ER and went home for recovery, she would feel better. But she didn't. Even a few days later she didn't change her mind about your mom going to Gainesville. She was adamant about having your mom stay with her.

"My mom tried to explain to her about the competition, even offering to stay with her while your mom was away. But"—Nahrin's voice turned low—"it seemed that your grandma didn't understand. All she talked about was how if her daughter wasn't with her, then things might go wrong. Like her arm might fall off or something. Then my mom offered to have me stay with her, and again she said no. The only person she wanted was your mom."

"Wow," I said again. "But why didn't you just talk to her, Mom?"

We all looked at my mother, but she wouldn't say anything.

"So our school couldn't go to the state championship," Nahrin continued. "A lot of people were mad at your mom, but I just felt bad for her. She didn't even bother to explain to her team or the coach or the principal why she couldn't go. She didn't care if they understood or not. All that mattered to her was her mother. And that was when I fell in love with her." Nahrin, seeming satisfied, stretched out his arms on the back of the booth.

"That's a very nice story," I said, smiling. Then I looked away. I should have been grateful that his story filled in that hole that had been growing since I met him. But I wasn't, because other holes began to form.

I knew that my mother loved my grandmother.

There'd been no denying my mother's affection when she stroked Grandma's back or when she came running down the stairs after Grandma screamed. Her friends knew this. Even the usher at the movie theater knew. Nahrin and Chet knew, too. It was apparent in her face. And it was for this reason—one that I would never tell anyone, not even Tracy—that I was a little glad that my grandmother had died. Did people know that my mother loved me, also? Was her reason for loving me more than the simple fact that she was my mother? Was this love—the one she had for me—obvious to everyone, as well?

Nahrin pulled out of the restaurant's parking lot and turned onto a big road where all of the businesses along the wide streets were parts of big chains. Walgreens. Home Depot. Chevron. Mom took out the shopping list that *Oum* Palla had given her for Grandma's funeral, and told Nahrin that we needed to go to an Asian store first. From what I understood, there were a lot of things that we needed to buy that evening to give to the temple for the funeral.

"We don't have any Asian stores in Scottsville," I reported from the backseat. "There are a couple of them in the Strip. But that's in the big city."

"When your mom and I came to St. Petersburg, there was only one Asian store. It was a Thai store. Remember, Chandra?" Nahrin asked Mom. Then to me he said, "Grace, your grandma loved these preserved bananas." He wanted to tell me the name of them but couldn't think of it. "Anyway, none of us had money when we arrived in

America. I think it was cheaper to buy fresh bananas from Albertsons, but your grandma didn't want those. She saved her pennies and nickels for a month just to buy these packaged bananas from the Thai market. They were a dollar twenty-nine a packet. Or something like that."

"A dollar and twenty-nine cents?" Chet said. He seemed as appalled as I was that it would take Grandma a whole month to save up that small amount.

"Man, Chet, you don't know," his brother said. "When you were born, Mom and Dad had a little bit of money. You didn't have to wear the same pair of socks for three days. You grew up in a nice house, with your own room, and new clothes to wear. Man, you had it made."

I thought Chet would have something smart to come back with, but he didn't.

We went to the same Asian store that Mom and I had visited a couple of days earlier. Nahrin studied the list Mom was holding and found the short, pouty woman who didn't smile, and said to her in English, "I need a box of bittermelons. Do you have it?"

"Bittermelon?" the woman asked.

"Yes, it's long and green. And it's bitter."

To me the green, bumpy vegetable tasted like medicine, and I couldn't understand why Grandma had liked it. She sometimes bought the sliced dehydrated ones at Lotus Supermarket and boiled them, drinking the bitter green tea whenever she had a temperature.

The woman nodded ferociously, and I couldn't tell if she appreciated the business or if she was annoyed at the special request. "Yes, yes, I know bittermelon."

188

"Well, do you have a lot of them? I will need a boxful."
Nahrin pantomimed the perimeter of a box with his arms.

"No today. When you want?"

"As soon as possible. When can you get them?"

The woman went to the back of the store and talked to a man. When she returned, she told us that she would get the melons in on Thursday. Nahrin and Mom were satisfied and gave the woman his number.

Before we left the store, we purchased for Grandma's funeral ten packages of rice noodles; two boxes of egg noodles (each holding thirty individual-size packs); three sacks of jasmine rice; five packets of dried fish from the freezer; five cans each of jackfruits and longans; five boxes each of incense sticks and candles; two heavy, furry blankets, one with prints of flowers and the other with the head of a tiger; and two packets of green mung beans.

Our next stop was Jo-Ann Fabrics. Chet and I followed Nahrin and Mom as they circled around the iron racks of silk, cotton, and chiffon. A lady walked up to Mom and asked if she needed help. "I need fourteen yards of this, please," my mother said, and pulled out a bolt of white cotton fabric.

At Target, Chet and I went to Food Avenue Express while his brother and my mother finished shopping for Grandma's funeral.

Chet ordered a slice of pepperoni pizza and a medium Coke, and we found a table near a trash can.

I picked a pepperoni off his pizza. "So, are you going to tell me? What did you find out?"

The night before, after Maly and *Meing* Huor had left,

he'd said that he'd found my dad in a yearbook. My father had gone to school on the south side of the city. From the yearbook, Chet was able to identify the Cambodians that he might have hung out with. There was a guy in there that Chet remembered seeing his brother playing basketball with on a couple of occasions. He'd told me that he was going to call the basketball friend and ask him about my dad this morning.

Now he asked, "What are you talking about?"

I kicked him under the table. "You know what."

"I know, I know." He put down his pizza. "Okay."

I sat up in my chair. His skin was very smooth looking, making me wonder what it would feel like to touch his cheeks. His eyes were steady and serious. Even though we were sitting, he seemed tall and tough. Until then I'd never realized how square his jawline was. How the six-year difference between our ages could give him that much more wisdom. "Nahrin's friend knew your dad."

"I knew it!" I said.

Chet said that the friend had been able to answer all of his questions. My father's age. When he had come to the United States. Where he lived when Mom was a senior. And what happened to him not too long after. The friend also said that my father had only one family member left, an uncle named Son.

"Just one uncle?" I asked, sitting back in the chair. The number was so small.

"Yeah." Chet said that my dad and his uncle had come together from Cambodia as part of a group that Catholic

Charities sponsored. "I know it's not a large family like you wanted, but at least there's someone. Right?"

One was still a very lonely number, but he had a good point. "Yeah. One is better than nothing."

Chet nodded. "The guy doesn't know where your father's uncle is living now, but he will ask around."

"But what are we going to do if he doesn't find out? I'm leaving on Sunday."

"Chill, kid. We've gotten this far."

His confidence comforted me, and I took a sip of his Coke. Then I hit the table. "Oh my God. I have a picture of my dad. I want you to tell me if he'd changed much. I mean, of course there would be *some* changes, but—"

"You have a picture?" Chet asked.

"Yeah, I do." I opened my backpack and pulled out the scrapbook. Chet reached for it, and I slapped his hand. "Lay off. This is private." I opened it to the last page, and gently pulled my father out from the four stick-on corners. I showed Chet the picture. "This is my dad. See?"

Chet took the picture from me and studied it, his eyes darting between the man on the paper and me, over and over. "Grace," he finally said.

I closed my eyes and felt my neck turn hot. I didn't understand how my name, which was supposed to make a person see light and swans with soft slim necks and Roman goddesses wearing long, flowy white dresses, could be so full of bad news all the time.

"This isn't your dad."

I leaned in and took the photo back. "Yes, he is. My

grandmother told me. She gave him to me. She said that this is my father. See?" I pointed to the solemn-looking man in the picture.

Chet shook his head. I thought all his feelings had moved up to his throat, as I could see the side of it pulsing.

"This is my father," I said, feeling the burning in my eyes. "My grandmother told me that he is my father. She wouldn't have lied."

Chet put his hand on mine. "I don't think she lied. I don't think she meant to, anyway. But this is not your dad." He picked up the photo again. "This, I think, is your grandfather. See, it's an old photograph. Pictures used to look like this." He was pointing to the white scalloped edges. He also pointed to the torn corner, and ran his finger across the picture to show me how faded it had become over the years. I watched his thin long finger brushing over my grandfather. My grandfather who had died as a soldier. Was my grandmother finally with him now, along with their second daughter? And possibly my father? Were they all looking down at my mother and me and hoping for the best for us?

I remember wanting to smack Chet. And wanting to be near him, too. I didn't understand why. I just knew that when your mind and heart were in a civil war, you got a headache that filled up your head and threatened to pop.

Chet was right. Of course he was. Grandma had been confused when she showed me the picture, just as she was confused that a Fourth of July celebration was a combat zone. That was why when I later asked her about my dad's picture, she didn't know what I was talking about. I saw again the day she had told me about the Khmer Rouge eating human liver. Now I understood that Pol Pot had been a time period that my grandmother had had to cross. She had made it over that border, but she was lost in the new land.

I took the picture back from Chet and carefully put it back in my scrapbook. "Sometimes I don't think I'm supposed to be here. Do you know what I mean?"

He didn't.

"I have a lot of friends. You know, I'm pretty cool at school, but I'm alone," I said. "Not lonely, but alone."

Chet patted my hand, and as much as I liked the warmth of his palm and fingers, I pulled away. I didn't know why his touch made me feel so empty. Was this why Mom had snuck her hand out from underneath Nahrin's at the restaurant? How odd that a human touch could isolate you as well as comfort you.

"You're not alone. You have me. You have your mom."

"My mom didn't want me. Did she ever tell you guys? She did it with my dad because she was mad at my grandmother."

"Well, I don't think all parents want their kids all the time. You know what I mean? That would be too much, too utopia."

I turned away. "I hate it when people analyze what I say."

Chet said that he hadn't meant to get all educated on me.

"I knew this kid who had to see a chiropractor three times a week because he couldn't walk straight," I said. "It had to do with his back and shoulders. The doctor said

193

that the kid had put too much weight on one shoulder, and that was why he was walking lopsided. I feel like that. Lopsided, like I'm about to fall over. My mom told me that she didn't love my dad. I'm learning to accept that. What I want to know, though, is if he loved her. And I want to know if he would have fought to keep me once he laid his eyes on me."

"Grace," Chet said.

"Please don't say my name."

He folded his hands into a ball on the table.

"There are other things about my dad that I want to know. Like if I got these crooked pinkies from him. And if so, did he get his from his parents. Because if he did, chances are that my kids would get them, too, you know. I want to be able to tell them things like this. I don't want strangers to know more about my family than I do. So I just want to know him, that's all."

A kid tripped near our table, and Chet helped him up.

"Your brother was right. You have the perfect life. Your mom, dad, and brother, to balance things out. How it's supposed to be."

"You know your mom, and you knew your grandma," Chet said.

"My grandma is gone, and she was not my father."

Chet said he was sorry.

That night I found Mom sitting on the springless bed, in her pajamas, staring out the window, still holding the shopping list in her right hand. She hadn't washed her face, and part of her hair was in a ponytail and the other part just hung down the side of her cheek. I went to my backpack and took out my scrapbook, opening it to the fourth page and handing it to her.

"What's this?" she asked. "I thought it was your journal."

"It is. But you can look at it."

She took my scrapbook, appearing confused as she saw Tom Hanks. It was one of my favorite pictures of him. In it he wore a clean white undershirt and dark blue jeans. Very casual, very "I'm a corporate man, but today I'm working in the yard."

Mom turned more pages, quickly perusing my collection. She glanced up at me. Her lips were dry and had only a remnant of a lip liner. "You have a lot of photographs."

"Yeah. I've had the book for a while. You know, a picture here and a picture there."

"Grace," my mother said.

I looked down at the gray carpet and asked, "Yes?"

"These pictures are only of men."

"They're actors."

She turned more pages. "I didn't think it was a big deal that you liked Tom Selleck, but you seem to like all of these older men."

"They are movie actors, Mom. The ones that I think have merits."

"But where are the female actors that you think have merits?"

I took the scrapbook and looked down at my feet, red in the face. I did not want a lecture on the proper way to collect pictures of celebrities. For that brief time, I just wanted, *needed*, her to understand me. "I have pictures of women," I lied to her. "I just haven't had time to put them in here."

"Well—"

"Wait, Mom," I said. "Please, just look, okay?"

She flipped through the pages, and finally we got to the last one. I pulled out the picture of my grandfather and handed it to her. She took it from me. As she gazed at her father, I couldn't decide if I should give her privacy. It was personal, seeing your father again after so long. Would she want anyone to watch her?

I headed for the door when Mom sighed a deep, "Wow. Where did you get this?"

"Grandma. She gave it to me. I think she meant to give it to you, but she got mixed up. You know, like she did about many things."

Mom cradled her father in her hand. "We don't have any pictures of us back then. I forgot she had hidden this during Pol Pot. I've seen it before, but it was a long time ago and I'd completely forgotten what he looked like."

"Well, he died when you were so young, Mom. Of course you would forget."

She held the faded black-and-white photo to her chest. "If your own children don't remember you, who will? How horrible it must be to have lived but to have no one remember your face when you die. It's almost as if you've never existed." Her eyes reddened, the tears brimming at the lashes, and she bit her lips. Then the tears began to fall, and I could almost hear them hitting her thighs, one by one. I reached out to touch her, but she shook her head, and I held my hand behind my back. "I don't think that it's fair for some people to go down in history in every book that's ever been written and have the whole world know them, and that some people can't even be remembered by their children. Don't you think that there should be one long wall that spans the earth so that everyone who has died gets to have his or her picture posted on it? So that years and years from now, their children and grand-children can walk by it and say, 'Oh, yeah, I know her'?"

"Yes," I said.

"I was wrong, Grace, to not tell you about your father sooner. To not tell you about things sooner. But . . . it just hurt so much."

"You can tell me now," I said.

Mom got off the bed, found a tissue in her purse, and cleaned her face with it. "What *Bang* Nahrin said at dinner was right. When your grandma and I came to the United States, it was just the two of us." Her voice was so achingly far and distant I had to strain my ears to hear her. "*Oum* Palla helped us as much as she could, but she had her fam-ily to take care of. So your grandma and I were like a pair of shoes. We completed each other.

"It was important to her that I did everything right, Grace. According to her the community was always watch-ing. She taught me to *chumreap suor* the adults. To not dance or sing at dinnertime. To wash the laundry. To clean the house. To cook rice. I did those things, and she didn't date. It was like a pact she made for us."

Mom cleared her throat and spoke a little louder. "Your grandma knew that Nahrin and I were in love. But because she was very strict, he and I weren't allowed to have a relationship that was more than the sister-brother one. For a long time I respected her opinion. But when she didn't let him take me to my prom, things started to change for me. I started seeing things differently. I just didn't understand some of the things that she believed were so important. It was only a dance, and he and I were going to get married someday, anyway. But it wasn't the dance that upset me, you know?" Mom stared into my eyes. "I had done everything for her. Do you know how hard that was? How tiring?"

She waited for my answer, but I knew not to say anything out loud. So in my mind I said, *I know now.*

"After that night with your father, I was scared. But after the home pregnancy test came out positive, I wanted to tell your grandmother first, Grace. Not Nahrin, not Maly. I wanted to tell your grandma because she was my mother, and something inside of me told me that she would know the right thing to do. But I was so wrong. The first thing your grandmother did was ask if Nahrin knew. I told her no. Then she wanted to know if I'd told anyone else. I said no again. She asked over and over if I'd told your dad. And again I said no. She seemed so relieved with my answers. And that confused me. I didn't understand why no one knowing about the pregnancy was that important to her. But what she did later confused me even more.

"In about a month we sold the house and packed a small U-Haul with some of our belongings. We told some people we knew that we were moving to Atlanta for my college. But on the day we left, we didn't even say good-bye to anyone. And we didn't go to Atlanta, either. That was just a lie. We didn't even know where we were going. There were too many Cambodians in Georgia, so your grandma had known not to go there. We went all the way to Pittsburgh because we had met someone at a rest stop who told us that Pittsburgh had good universities, for me, and many jobs, for her. The person said that there were many Asians in the area, but no Cambodians. So your grandma thought Pittsburgh would be perfect. And that's how we ended up there." Mom's eyes begged me to understand.

"Yeah, Mom," I said. "But Grandma wanted to come back. You didn't."

"I know, I know. And that's why she blamed me for her sad life! But, Grace, your grandma was the one who moved us. She was so ashamed of me that she couldn't face her friends. And I couldn't just move back because she was ready. She didn't even let me tell Nahrin the truth before we moved. I left him like I'd never cared about him. How could I face him and pretend that nothing happened?" She blew into the tissue. "Your grandma could have let me tell Nahrin, you know; maybe he would have loved me still. But she didn't care about any of that. Just about herself. I did one thing that she had told me not to, and it was like she stopped loving me. I just didn't understand why she chose the community over me!"

She held on to the dresser, and her body shook as she continued to weep. I wanted desperately to tell her that I understood her now, that I understood perfectly that she had felt unloved by her mother. I wanted, too, to tell her that she had it all wrong. Grandma may have been ashamed and embarrassed, but she had chosen her over the community; that was why Grandma had taken her and run. I got up off the bed to touch my mother.

Mom stuck her hand out at me and said, "Don't." And I sat back down on the bed.

When her shoulders stopped shaking, and it seemed that there were no more tears inside of her screaming to gush out, I could only say, "I'm sorry."

She ran a new tissue across her eyes and said, "I am, too." Then she held the old picture up again, studying her father's every feature. "Don't you want to keep this?"

"No, he's your father."

My mother put the picture inside her purse and sat on the carpet, among the new clothes that she'd had to buy for us. She began to fold some shorts and placed them in a pile, once in a while blowing her nose into the tissues. "Tomorrow I'm going back to the temple to help those old ladies with arranging the pantry. They think I will help them come up with a plan to make things easier to locate. You can come with me if you want." She picked up the black dress she'd bought for the wedding reception, and checked the stitching in it.

"You'll look good in it, Mom. You're hot. Hotter than *Bang* Maly."

"I don't care about that," she said.

Mom wanted to see if our suitcase would be big enough to hold all our belongings, and she began to pack it. It was only a little larger than a carry-on size, and it was already full with just our shorts and some of our tops. Mom must have not noticed what I had, though. She got on her knees and began to push underwear and the rest of our shirts into the outside pockets of the suitcase, and she continued to jam our socks and her schoolbooks into the inside. When she was satisfied that she'd packed everything, she tried to close the lid of the suitcase but couldn't, and it sat on top of the books like the top lip of an opened mouth. Mom stood up and stepped on the suitcase and pressed down on it. But it would not shut, and one of the shoes fell out. Then, out of nowhere, she stomped on the suitcase, over and over, before she kicked it.

The suitcase did not go far. But the other shoe, the books, and a couple of shirts fell out.

I got up off the bed again, and this time I stood beside our poor suitcase. "It's okay," I said to her. "It'll be over after this Sunday, like you said."

Mom snorted at me, her eyes puffy now. "You know, Grace, I'm not doing this funeral because I'm afraid your grandma is going to haunt me. I'm not scared of things like that."

"Oh, I know. *Oum* Palla said you're doing it because it's the right thing."

As Mom stood straight and tall in front of me with question marks all over her face, I knew that I'd never been more of a disappointment to her. "But what is the right thing?" she said. "Is the right thing doing what's been done, what's been told to you? It's a funeral, Grace. Don't you think there has to be a better reason for doing it, other than because it is the right thing?"

12

Nahrin dropped Mom and me off at the temple on Wednesday morning before he went to work. Mom's eyes were still puffy from crying the night before, and she wore extra concealer to mask the redness and tenderness. She did not want to go to temple that morning but told Nahrin that she had to. "I want to make sure that they will come on Sunday for the funeral," she had said.

As soon as we walked through the front door, I smelled rice cooking and incense sticks burning. Freshly cooked rice reminded me of the smell of rain, and combined with the incense sticks, the temple that day gave the scent of both new and old. Four ladies in sheer sleeveless shirts, with wrinkled, sagging skin on their arms and faces, were sitting on woven plastic mats on the floor. Unlike my grandmother, these women were truly old because of their age and not because of their health. They were polishing large silver bowls and platters.

"Chandra, Grandchild Chandra," one of them said in Cambodian to my mother. It was the lady with the big ears who we had spoken to at temple only a few days earlier. She extended her arms, and Mom slowly went in to hug her.

The rest of the old women wanted hugs from my mother, and she obliged them, too, after she *chumreap suor*-ed them.

"Sit, sit," they said to us.

Mom hesitated before joining them in the circle. After she sat for a while, she nervously thanked them. Then she and the old women just sat and smiled at one another. As I observed everyone, I didn't know who was more uncomfortable: Mom, who was the center of attention but was without words, or I, who felt as though I were merely an extension of my mother.

After the old women drank in Mom's beautiful made-up face with the sad eyes, the careful jewelry she'd selected for her ears and wrist, and her soft, lotioned hands, they finally acknowledged me.

"You look just like your mother when she was little," a lady said.

I thanked her.

Then they went back to adoring my mother. "Remember, Chandra, you and your mom slept in temple some nights. And at night you stayed up reading until the monk sent you to bed," Big-Eared Lady said.

"*Chas, Chas,*" Mom said.

"Oh, that monk cherished you like no other little girl," another woman said. She rubbed a dried leaf with a red paste, folded it over and over until it was the size of a nickel, and pushed it into the side of her mouth. Moments later the corners of her mouth were etched with remnants of the red juice. The lady sitting beside her had more stories to tell about my mother, and slowly Mom began to fill in missing parts even when they hadn't asked her to. But for the most part she sat back, her face taking on that glow that I'd never managed to kindle in her.

Two of them kidded with Mom and asked her to dance for them again, like she had when she was a little girl. An old man walked into the room and teased her in Cambodian, "We'll give you quarters for it."

"She's grown and is a teacher, with a beautiful daughter, so what is she going to do with your quarters, Grandpa?" Betel-Juice Lady asked him.

"Oh, *Yeay,*" he said, "no one can joke around you." Then he walked back toward where he had just come from.

"So," the fourth old woman said. Until then she hadn't said anything. She was tiny, about my grandma's size, and she was cute like a baby but appeared undeniably wise. Her shaved head was beautifully round, and I just wanted to hold it in my hands. "How was your mother? Before she *slab*?" she asked Mom gently.

The room turned quiet, and all old four ladies looked at Mom again, their eyes beseeching her to share, share. I could tell that my mother was thinking; her eyes held that distant look that I knew so well. And I was wondering if she was feeling the way I had at our house when Tif asked about my grandmother's last day. I wondered how she would hide her true feelings from these women who obviously cherished her, but whom she also blamed for having sent her and her mother away.

"*Yeay,*" my mother said sadly and slowly, "I don't know. I don't think she was very happy."

Someone sighed regretfully.

"Your mother tried so hard. She never rested. She had such a sad life," Big-Eared Lady said.

"Well, even when Naree was here, she wasn't very happy." It was the lady who had said I looked like my mother. "She always had a worried face. Could never relax. It was in her nature to be sad."

"She wasn't sad all the time," my mother said defensively. "Being sad and having a sad life are different from each other. A person can be sad for one day, but that doesn't mean she had a sad life. My mother did not have a sad life. One day she was singing in the rain."

"Singing in the rain? No. A grown woman?" Betel-Juice Lady asked.

"Yes," Mom said firmly. And the old ladies looked at her for the details, seeming to still not believe her. "It was when my daughter was five years old," my mother began.

Mom was talking about a Saturday afternoon a couple of months after we had moved into the new house, after the large photograph had been put up. Outside, raindrops were hitting our roof and windows like rocks. Mom was napping upstairs. Grandma and I were watching one of her favorite old shows downstairs, and we fell asleep, too, on the couch. When we woke up, it was still raining. But the sun was out, and the sky was one of those blues that made you believe everything was okay.

Grandma put me in my red and white polka-dot bathing suit and took me outside. She had grabbed a section of the newspaper from the kitchen. As we stood under our front porch, she made a sailboat from the black and white paper. Then we walked the few steps to the sidewalk with our boat and squatted down in the rain. Her shirt was wet almost instantly, and I could see the pear shapes of her breasts. She brushed the water off her face and set the boat in the gutter, where rainwater had already collected, and we watched our sailboat sail down to the next house before it got too wet and deflated.

I stayed on the sidewalk as Grandma continued to bring me fresh boats, and as I set each one asail I jumped and clapped. My grandmother became so excited with her creations that she started running down the sidewalk, her hands waving in the air. She sang that the cold water felt good. Seeing her in such a delirium, I ran up and down, too, until Mom stuck her head out of her bedroom window and yelled down at us.

I stopped in my tracks, scared that my grandmother and I were in trouble. But Grandma was lost in her own world as she continued to dance up and down the sidewalk, singing about the rain.

"I'll go get her," I yelled up to Mom. But she was not at her window anymore.

I ran to my grandmother, grabbed her arm, and started

to pull her back to our house. But she was stronger than I thought, and I couldn't get her to move. "Come on, Grandma. Mom's awake. She doesn't want you out here," I pleaded.

My grandmother didn't seem to hear a single word I was saying. The drops hit her in the face, and she opened her mouth to swallow them.

"Please, come on, Grandma. Come on," I begged, fearing that at any minute my mother was going to storm out of the house and order us inside like bad children.

But as I held my grandmother's wrist in my small hand, I looked at our front porch again, and there, standing on the bottom step of it, was Mom, in a tank top and shorts, barefoot. Her legs and chest were already wet. And to my surprise, she was laughing, her upper body shaking back and forth, and waving a sailboat at us.

For the next half hour, Grandma continued skipping up and down the sidewalk as Mom continued to make me my paper sailboats. "Look at your grandma," Mom said. "Look how happy and free she is. I wish it was always this easy."

I did as my mother said that day. I looked. I looked at both my grandmother and my mother, wishing, too, it was always that easy for all three of us.

"Well," Big-Eared Lady said after Mom finished the story, "if I were brave like your mom, I would run out and sing in the rain, too."

"And if I were young, I would do it naked," Beautiful-Head Lady said.

Betel-Juice Lady jabbed her in the rib. "You talk so inappropriately. Look at Chandra's daughter. She's embarrassed now."

They all turned their attention to me again, and I quickly donned my coy face.

"You were a good daughter, Chandra," Long-Eared Lady said. "You took good care of your mom."

Mom's eyes teared up again. "No, I wasn't."

Big-Eared Lady leaned into my mother. "Young or old, who doesn't make mistakes?"

In the afternoon several more old ladies and men dropped by the temple. One man, with dark wavy hair, asked Mom about Sunday. He wanted to build a procession into the service; she told him that whatever he thought should be done, should. She also told him the date of Grandma's death and when she had been cremated. The man explained to Mom that it would be very important for her to do another ceremony in honor of Grandma one hundred days after her death. Mom said that she would and that she would also give *Oum* Palla some money to bring food to temple on the one-hundred-day anniversary.

As Mom wiped the framed pictures in the large room, Betel-Juice Lady said morosely to her, "Oh, Chandra. Why do you live in a place with no Khmers? Come back here."

My mother softly explained that someday she would return, but not right then. Another old lady asked, "But your mother's ashes will be here. How are you going to *sain*?"

A woman from across the large room screeched, "You can do that anywhere. You don't need a temple to *tweu bouhn* for your mother. You don't need a temple to show your mother gratitude." Everyone agreed.

After we ate lunch with the old women and old men, Mom couldn't find the mops, but she did find a bucket and a couple of rags in a hall closet. She poured some bleach into the pail and filled it halfway with hot water. Then she handed me a rag, and we walked to the far end of the room.

I'd never touched a floor before, except for an occasional sweeping; at home my chores were to keep my and Grandma's room clean and to pick up after myself. So when Mom told me to scrub the new tile floor by hand, I was kind of lost. I watched her soak the rag in the hot water, wring out the excess liquid, and run the rag back and forth on the floor, a small section at a time. Once I got the hang of it, I liked the job. I was proud to be able to wipe off scuff marks on the tiles and make them look new, like a clean canvas.

While Mom scrubbed beside me, we did not speak. Even though she was there physically, doing what I was doing, I knew that her mind and heart were in a different place. At the time, I was happy for her, happy to hear her hum to herself while moving water around on the cool floor. But now, looking back at that day, as I have learned to do with most days of my life, I can say that I was quiet at temple because I had accepted something about my mother and me.

After Big-Eared Lady had spoken to her that morning at the temple, my mother had become different. There was no ignoring that my mother's shoulders had relaxed during lunch and that her steps later in the kitchen when she was putting away the dishes had been soft and quiet.

Even though Beautiful-Head Lady was my favorite at temple that day, I truly admired Big-Eared Lady. When it came down to people like her, I believed that wisdom really did come with age. What she had said to my mom was simple and was not convoluted like the lectures my teachers had given us about fallen European empires or American writers. My mother had been wrong. My grand-mother had been wrong. Everyone who played a role in my grandmother's taking my mother away had been wrong. Reassuring my mother that she was not responsible for Grandma's discontentment had brought the relief that she had been searching for. But more than that, in Big-Eared Lady's statement there had been an apology to my mother. It was vague, and whom the apology was from was really not known. But it didn't matter. What mattered was that it was there for my mother to take. And I wondered, *Why couldn't I have thought to offer her that?*

I realized that *Oum* Palla and Chet and *Meing* Huor and these old ladies loved my mother. And every one of those people was able to give her something that she yearned for: an acceptance of her past and everything that came with it, including her mistakes and imperfections. The only thing I was able to offer her was the present, something she wasn't craving. And unlike before, when I would jump at anything to please my mother, that day I was beginning to understand that I might never be able to give her what she needed.

13

I woke up early the next morning, to *Oum* Palla's booming loud voice from the kitchen. "Yes, yes, it's this Sunday," she said in Cambodian into the phone. "Of course, I know you don't know her. But you can still come. Yes, the day after Maly's wedding. Well, don't drink so much then." She laughed her carefree laugh and hung up the phone. I wondered if Mom knew that *Oum* Palla was begging people to attend Grandma's service.

After *Oum* Palla finished her calls, I listened to the rain hitting the window like small pieces of glass, and the furious wind howling and thrashing through the tree branches. The sun peaked through the clouds for just seconds, glaring through the window and into the room for just as brief a time. Before Mom had left early that morning for temple again to work on the pantry, she had cursed the weather. She had asked if I wanted to go with her, and I told her no.

I was thinking about catching Chet before his classes to ask how everything was going with searching for my dad's uncle, when the doorbell rang.

"*Chumreap suor, chumreap suor,*" *Oum* Palla said to her guests. There were many voices, each of them speaking Cambodian when they entered the house, and a couple of them sounding familiar.

"You so pretty," one of them said to her. It was *Yeay* Mao.

I also recognized Maly's and David's voices, and listened to everyone trying to tell each other how they were doing. Then I heard a man's and a woman's, and they turned out to be Maly's in-laws. Were they here just to meet me?

I jumped out of bed and rummaged through the pile of new clothes for something unwrinkled.

David's parents started to talk about Seattle. They preferred their rainy city over sunny California for many reasons. As in California, there was a large Cambodian population, so it was a lot of fun around New Year and *Bouhn Phhum.* But Seattle was safer than California. They thought California was a fun place to visit, but not a safe place to raise kids. Too many gangs. Part of their family lived around Long Beach and called them regularly about the trouble their kids were getting into.

The conversation outside soon turned to the wedding, and everyone's voice became low. Moments later *Oum* Palla called for me. Then I heard the knock at the door and her telling me that the sun was out and the doorknob turning. I tried to hurry, but I couldn't find a top to match the running shorts I had been able to find.

"Grace?" *Oum* Palla whispered.

"Good morning," I said when I saw her. She wore fresh makeup, and her hair was pulled back in another bun. "I'm almost ready."

"Almost ready? *Bang* David's parents are here. They're here visiting, and they want to see you. Come on." She looked impatient.

"I can't go now, *Oum.* I'm not dressed. I haven't even combed my hair or brushed my teeth."

"Come on," she insisted. And to my surprise she pulled me up off the floor just as I was able to pull on the shorts. I yanked my thin cami down to cover my belly button. "Don't talk directly to anyone, and you'll be okay. And smooth your hair out of your face. It's amazing what we all truly look like without lotion and hair spray. And don't act like you just woke up. Girls don't sleep in this long."

"What about boys?" I asked as I followed her out of the guest room. My legs felt cold.

"Shush. And make sure you *chumreap suor* everyone," she whispered down my neck.

I stood beside the entertainment unit and smiled at the people on the sofa. Their faces were long, and no one seemed to have had a good night's rest. I crossed my ankles, and then uncrossed them when I noticed *Oum* Palla staring at my feet. I crossed my arms around my chest, too, and then uncrossed them when she stared at me and told her guests who I was. I clumsily folded my hands and *chumreap suor*-ed all six adults. *Oum* Palla laughed nervously and told me that I didn't have to *chumreap suor* her. *You're staying with me, and you don't have to* chumreap suor *people you live with,* she seemed to say to me. *Don't you know?*

"Oh," I said. I grinned, but no one's expression changed. Maly especially didn't look pleased. Were they here to tell me the wedding was off?

I felt my nipples hardening under my thin top as I thought about what I was wearing in front of these people. I hoped no one would look at my butt when I walked away. Why hadn't I insisted on putting on a shirt first? I slouched over, folded my arms around myself, and bent at the knees, to cover myself.

"Where you visiting from?" David's mom asked me in broken English. She was a petite woman with short curly hair and a stoic face. Her eyebrows were precisely plucked and arched in a semicircle above her eyeglasses.

I cleared my throat and told her Scottsville.

"Scott-will?" she asked with a frown. She was wearing a lilac-colored suit, and she held her dark purple handbag on her knees, running her fingers along it when she asked, "Where that?"

"Uh," I said, "around Pittsburgh. In Pennsylvania?" *In Pennsylvania?* I almost hit myself for sounding so dumb.

"It snows there, right?"

I turned to the wide-shouldered man. His voice was piercing and lazy at the same time, and he sat up very erect. He had a large, box-shaped head covered with beautiful white hair. His long eyebrows were as white as the feathers of a bird's underbelly, and they swept into his small, squinting eyes that were pulled down by the baggy pouches underneath them.

I answered David's father, "Yes, it does."

"A lot?" he grunted.

I showed all of them with my hand how high snow could get in Scottsville. Everyone but David's parents seemed amazed by it.

"Where your mom?" David's mom asked. I told her that she was helping at the temple. "Where your dad?" I told her that he had passed away. "And your grandparents?" I told them that my grandfather had passed away during Pol Pot and that my grandmother had passed away, too, but only about three weeks ago. "From what?" she asked.

I didn't understand why she was asking all of these questions that made me see my grandmother running around with a large towel around her head or my dad sinking into the bottom of an ocean. It occurred to me then that I had forgotten to ask when his body was found. I must have scrunched up my face in confusion, since David answered for me. "It's okay, Mother," he said gently in Cambodian.

Maly looked down at her feet, and *Yeay* Mao and David's mother shared a glance at me. After I stood for several more minutes, feeling like a plucked chicken ready for steaming, boiling, baking, or pan-frying, *Oum* Palla told me that I could go.

Oum Palla knew to leave me alone later that morning when I was eating my cereal. And I hated it that she was so

215

smart. Instead of talking to me, she was busy cleaning out her cupboards. Cleaning the freakin' cupboards! At the dining table I was pretending to enjoy the sound of flakes crunching in my mouth, the rain hitting the roof and window like bullets now, and the boring newspaper article about a bird that had saved a dog's life. I wished, though, she would say something just so I could tell her to shut up.

As I drank up the last drop of sugared milk in my bowl, Chet sauntered in and rubbed my hair. "You had a rough morning, huh, kid? Talking to those stiff and proper people."

Oum Palla told him to mind his own business. He sat at one end of the table and gloated.

"How do you know?" I asked.

He laughed and told me that he had heard everything from his room.

I glared at him. "You were home? Why didn't you have to come out and *chumreap suor* everyone!"

"Whoa." Chet held out his hands. "Don't get mad at me. I wasn't there."

I got up from my chair, with both fists on the table. "I know, stupid! I know you weren't there. That's why I asked why your mom didn't make you go out there and be humiliated, too."

"Don't yell in this house," *Oum* Palla sternly ordered, and slammed shut a cupboard door. I hated her so much. "Girls do not yell."

"And girls can't sleep in, either, right?"

"Don't talk to me in that tone, Grace."

I bit my lip and sat back down. "You don't care about

anyone but your kids," I growled. "You said you were my grandma's best friend. You and she slept together the night before your wedding. Do you think my grandmother would have wanted you to let people talk to me the way David's parents did? You should have at least tried to stop them. But you didn't do anything. You wouldn't have let that happen if someone talked to your precious Nahrin and Chet that way. I hate you." I got up again, to stare at *Oum* Palla.

Chet told me to quiet down. He must have known that his mother was beyond angry. He must have seen that her mouth was tight, her forehead was folded in two creases, and her cheeks were glowing with anger.

Oum Palla pointed at me as though her arm were an arrow and her finger were the arrowhead. "Sit down," she ordered, and threatened in Cambodian, "I'm not scared to hit you."

I sat down.

Several minutes passed before she said, "I am your family. Remember that, and remember that I would never intentionally betray your grandma." She walked closer to the table and stood just a foot from it. I stared at my bowl. "Would you have spoken disrespectfully to your grandma?"

"No," I answered softly.

"I hope not. She didn't raise her daughter to be rude, so I know she did not raise you any differently."

Chet and I were motionless. Me, because I was afraid. Chet, probably because he was afraid, too. Maybe he also felt that his mother would always have control over him. But, unlike me, he didn't seem to care.

"Now, what is your problem?" *Oum* Palla asked, in a voice that I was used to hearing from her.

"There's no problem," I mumbled, with my back to her.

"Oh, there's a problem. Because if there wasn't, I don't think you would have told me you hated me."

"I don't hate you," I said. "I hated how you made me stand in front of those mean people. I hated how they asked me questions the way they did and made me answer them. Like they were better than me." I couldn't tell her, though, that I hated how David's mom, with her matching suit and purse, professionally colored hair, and expensive makeup, looked. How she was so put together, so sure of herself, so intelligent. How my grandmother couldn't achieve such a thing.

"They're old. They can ask whatever they want," she said in Cambodian.

"But I can't? I'm almost an adult, but I know almost nothing. Shouldn't I be the one who gets to ask questions?"

Chet opened his eyes wide, as if begging me to stop talking back. And I gave him the ugliest face I could make.

"And why shouldn't they ask you questions?" *Oum* Palla sounded truly appalled. "They were questions about your family." *A family,* I thought, *in which except for three people, everyone is dead.* "Why would you hate someone for that?"

"You know what I mean."

"No, I don't. You wanted to be in their son's wedding."

"Maly asked me. You heard her yourself. How can you say no to someone who wants you to be in her wedding? It would only be the biggest insult ever."

218

"Fine, but with that comes challenges. And that's just something you have to deal with," she said, then stopped, catching her breath. "David's parents wanted to meet you. I think their request was not out of the ordinary, to know about you and your family. You should be proud of your grandmother," *Oum* Palla said, in a sound close to a whisper. "She had a very hard life."

"Yeah, but if she had learned English like you and your husband, it wouldn't have been so hard for her," I said. "Then—"

"Grace!" *Oum* Palla snapped.

"I mean—"

"Didn't you hear any of the things I've been telling you?"

"I know. But—"

"She was smart, Grace. Your grandmother was smart inside."

"Yep, Grace," Chet echoed, "your grandmother was smart inside."

Oum Palla shot her eyes at Chet and told him to shut up.

"I was being—" he started to say, his voice feeble and defenseless all of a sudden.

"Shut up," she said again.

We were completely drowned in silence. I heard the humming of her refrigerator; once in a while it let out a small burp. I wondered if Chet was occupying his time the same way I was, counting the number of burps. Surely he must have been as afraid as I was to speak. This was different from other times *Oum* Palla had told him to shut up. This time, she actually meant it.

"You kids who were born here don't know anything,"

Oum Palla began. "All you care about is how you want to live your life, with no regard for how your parents want to live theirs. You expect for us to just throw out everything that we knew and start over completely. Just like that. Close one book, and start on a new one."

"I—" I said.

"Be quiet, Grace. For a young girl, you talk too much." Her voice was now low and steady.

I shut up again and tried not to let my breath be heard. It was hard to hold the sounds in, though, just to show someone how respectful you actually were. I thought of my grandmother and how frustrating it must have been for her to hold so much of herself inside. I used to hate it in school when I raised my hand to answer a question and the teacher didn't pick me. God, I did all I could just to not blurt out the sentences that I had put together in my head. And for Grandma, who must have had sentences in her own head, and not be able to blurt them out? Not because someone prohibited her from doing so, but because she couldn't translate her sentences into English ones? Oh, the agony of not being able to show the world who you really were!

"What's sad is that you young people would never understand how it was," *Oum* Palla said. "You're American. With what you know, you can go anywhere you want and feel that you're capable. You can go to a restaurant in Spain and order yourself a Coke or get on the Internet in England and order yourself running shoes. You will never know how it feels to have died and been reborn. You will never know how it is to come to a new country with nothing but the clothes you have on and the papers you are made to carry in a plastic bag to tell the Americans who you are. You don't have anything else, not even pictures of yourself, from the land you left. They were all lost or burned up during Pol Pot. And when you get here, you see everyone walking around you in different directions like live chickens. And you hope that this feeling of isolation is only temporary.

"But a week goes by and a month, and some more months. And you still feel like a lost dog. And one day you ask yourself, 'How am I going to cross the road without the cars hitting me?' And as you're thinking this, your little girl pulls your arm and leads you to the other side of the street. And when you're safe you realize that not a single car honked its damn horn at you. And then you're happy—and sad—all at once. You're here because of someone else. You only made it alive because of your daughter. The thought of her had kept you alive during Pol Pot. And now only she will keep you alive in this world that is as strange and faraway as the stars themselves. So you know that you will owe your life to her, forever.

"And to repay her, you buy her milk and cereal with all the food stamps they give you, and with the pennies that you find and save you buy yourself preserved bananas. And instead of going to night school to learn English for yourself, you clean toilets for cash, which you hide in your underwear because you're still unsure about banks. All of this forces you to say to yourself, 'So what if my daughter has to explain to the doctor about my irregular periods or pretends to be me on the phone.'

"And when they stop giving you free food, you find any job that will take someone who doesn't speak or write English, and you work without complaining. Because if you complain, they might fire you and hire someone who speaks and writes English. All day you feel as though someone's throwing bricks at your back, because you've been standing for eighty hours a week gluing electrical wires on an assembly line for the past year, because you're working two jobs, for your daughter. Because you know that a daughter isn't like a son. She will need special things. She needs to dress nicely, speak nicely, and be thought of nicely. You can't do anything that would put your daughter's future in jeopardy. You want others to know she came from a hardworking mother—not a family, mind you, because your community already knows your husband is gone. And to them, being without a husband is a handicap.

"So you do all you can to make up for what you don't have. Because you want someday for a nice, educated young man to marry your daughter. You know it's your responsibility to do everything now to help make that happen. And when you have time, you hope that everything you do now will mean something later when she looks at you one day and asks you why you're so needy and ignorant.

"Grace," *Oum* Palla finally said in Cambodian, "are you mad at me for saying these things to you? You're family. So I hope you aren't mad at me. From what I said, take what you want to hear, and throw the rest out. Okay, *Coan*?"

Even now, I'm not sure if people really know what shame is. Embarrassment I know everyone has felt. It stings and burns in your face like ant bites, and you wish those insects would dig a colony big enough for your body to be dragged to. Shame is different. It attacks your heart, spinning it over and over until you're dizzy and want to throw up everything that has made you a bad person so that you can be new again, like a freshly washed pitcher, all ready to be filled with clean water.

I did not answer *Oum* Palla that day, which seemed to have been the right decision. She kissed me on the head and said to her son, "Go pick up the bittermelons before your evening class." Then she said she had to take a nap. The funeral and the wedding were wearing her out.

Chet placed the box of green bittermelons in the trunk and hopped back into the driver's seat. He turned the radio to an R&B station and asked if I wanted to go anywhere. I told him that I didn't care.

The road was empty that rainy afternoon. There was a quietness to it that reminded me of snowstorm days in Scottsville. It was definitely exciting to be at school when the principal got on the intercom and explained to you the impending danger. But nothing compared to staying home later, where the furnace hummed, and your grandmother made you walk around in double socks and pushed you to eat her chicken and rice porridge. There was nothing like being safe with her, as the two of you looked out at the empty semiwhite streets, and at the white snow falling that etched the surrounding trees in white also. Or later when the two of you sat at the window, where it was cold and dark outside, the temperature in the twenties, but inside, huddled, you and she were so warm, and the sound of her laughing and giggling made you think, for that brief moment, life, with its screaming matches, silent treatments, and dancing in the rain, was the way it should be.

We drove on a windy road flanked by palm trees and listened to some guy singing about "getting it on" until we reached what Chet said was the destination, and I looked at the water on my right. He rounded the corner and parked across from a pink hotel circled by palm trees, with a large circular driveway at the front.

"You're okay?" he asked.

"Why wouldn't I be?"

He just sat there, leaving the car running, and the AC blew against my cheek as I looked out my window at the wide, treacherous water, water that could wipe you out in one bite. I saw the holes in my life, the water coming through them, filling me up, and sinking me. I was unable to shake off the questions in my head. How long had my father battled for his life in the water before he drowned? If he had seen me or held me, would he have fought harder, longer? Could I have saved him?

"Old people talk a lot sometimes," Chet said in a gentle voice. "They worry a lot. They just want to make sure their children turn out okay. So you just need to let them have their say. When they're done, they get tired, then they leave you alone. So don't let my mom—"

Before Chet could finish his sentence, I rose to my knees, and grabbed his jaw and held it in my hands, and I kissed him hard on his lips. I felt his hands on my arms, pushing me away, but that only made me press my face into his harder. He did not open his mouth like I wanted, so I sucked and bit his lips instead, until he threw me back, hard, and I hit my head on the window.

"Grace," Chet quickly said, "are you okay?" He reached for me, but I smacked him on the hand. He turned off the car and rolled down our windows about an inch each, and I rested my head against mine.

For the longest time, Chet and I sat in silence. And like other times, that silence was heavy and pressed down on me. I couldn't stop thinking of my father or my grandmother, of her small frame standing up for eighty hours of work a week. That was more than two weeks of school pushed into only one. I had wanted to come to this city for answers, for all the tiny pieces that would fill up all the holes within me. Instead, the holes multiplied. Maybe my mother was right. Maybe I asked too many questions. Maybe I should do as she had said—break free and live free—without attachments to pull me back with thoughts and worry and wonder. But I did wonder and worry, and I thought I always would. And this, I accepted, would forever keep me unfree.

"I . . . I . . . ," I said to Chet. "I'm sorry that I did that."

"Don't worry about it."

"I don't even like you that way."

"That's a relief," he said jokingly.

I said quietly, "I'm not mad at your mom." And I really wasn't. I knew she was a good person, she had to be. My own mother and grandmother trusted her.

"Good," Chet said. "She's nosy and pushy and all of those things, but she's a good woman."

"Don't you ever get mad at her, though? She's always saying you're stupid and lazy."

"Nah. She doesn't mean it."

I made a face at him. "Why don't you just tell her to lay off? It's your right."

"Why? What purpose would that serve, Grace?" He waited for me to answer, but I couldn't think of anything clever to say. "See? None. Except that my mother would be pissed off at me for offending her, and my brother would be pissed off at me for offending her, and then I would be pissed off at them for being offended. Piss would just be everywhere. Right? Nothing gets solved that way. It just gets too complicated sometimes when you try to bring an American rule into a Cambodian world. Sometimes it's just better to leave them apart."

"Whatever," I said. "What happened to your girlfriend, anyway?"

"Nothing," he answered. "Girls, they play so many games."

I sat up, as though I was insulted on behalf of womanhood. "Excuse me?"

"She goes out with her friends all day and pretends to try to call me later. I'm tired of it." By the somber look on his face, I thought he really was.

I wiped condensation off my window and stared out at the water again. The rain made it look gray and so far away. It was probably around here that my mother and father had created me. Had it taken them long? I rolled down my window, stuck my head out, and sucked in the air.

Chet said my name. And for once, it was beautiful to hear.

I turned to look at him. "Yeah?"

He reached into his back pocket and handed me a small sheet of yellow lined paper. "That's your great-uncle—Son Hang—and his address."

The paper felt so light in my hand, too light to hold the name of my great-uncle and his zip code. "Really?"

"Yep."

I held the paper in my fist, still not believing it.

"You know," he said, "I think your dad was a decent guy."

"Well, yeah. I'm sure my dad was a good guy. But what made you say that?"

"He didn't tell anyone he and your mom were together, you know what I mean? He's a guy. I'm a guy. Sometimes we start fooling around and we start talking, too. He could have said a lot about your mom, but he didn't."

I realized what Chet was getting at. My dad, for whatever reason he had had, had not told his friends how he "scored" with my mother, he hadn't risked shaming her and her mother. I put the small piece of paper in my backpack and thanked Chet.

"I hope it will give you what you need," he said.

I wasn't going to get my father, but at least I was still going to get parts of myself. "Oh, I know it will."

Chet pointed to the hotel. "I brought you here because I wanted to show you this place," he said. "I wish it was a nicer day, then we could take a walk. The hotel is famous. Anyone with money comes to the Vinoy."

I admired the handsome windows and balconies, the

tall palms. Chet told me that when his family first saw it, the Vinoy hadn't looked anything like it did now. At one time, before his family came to the United States, the hotel had been well known, but because of money issues it had ceased to operate. The original Vinoy became run-down, the windows and doors broken, homeless people sleeping in the dilapidated building. I couldn't picture what he said. All I could imagine were the Donald Trumps and Oprah Winfreys sashaying through the building.

"Nahrin told me that when he was a kid, all the adults would tell ghost stories about it."

"What did they say?" I asked.

Like me, Chet had his face turned to the hotel as he spoke. "They said that one night a woman found her husband cheating on her. So she killed him, and then later she killed herself with poison. And when she died, she came back each night, haunting the visitors. It was like she couldn't let go of what had happened. So she just hung around. And the visitors would check out early and never return. And soon, no one came."

I thought of the betrayed wife. "Do you think that's true?"

"I don't know. It's not like I asked my teachers and neighbors about it, and I don't think Nahrin did, either."

"What about the news? If it really happened, it would have been on the news."

Chet shrugged. "My family didn't really watch the news then. And they didn't read the newspaper, either. My parents depended on their friends for the news, and their friends depended on them, and kids like Nahrin, they just heard about what went on from all of them."

"I think it would be very easy to find out about the hotel on the Internet. We could Google it."

Chet said that he did realize that, but that he didn't want to. He moved in his seat and faced me. "I don't want to change what we knew back then," he said seriously. "My mom calls me the American Kid all the time, but I don't think my brother and I are very different. He was born in Cambodia, but both he and I grew up here, with parents who didn't know much about America. For sure, I appreciate how far we've come. But sometimes I think I'm too American. That's cool, don't get me wrong. I mean, think of a tree." He held out his arms in crooked ways as a prop. "All branches stick out from a tree, right? The leaves, they grow like crazy. Each year, the tree gets bigger and bigger. For me, being an American is like that—I'm the long branches, spreading out and taking over space. But, if you think about it, where do all of those branches lead back to? One place: the trunk. Rooted in the ground. I don't want to forget how I got here. Do you know what I mean?"

"Yes, *Bang* Chet," I said. "Yes, I understand perfectly."

14

As soon as I saw the taxi pull up in front of the iron mailbox, I went through the back door of the house, shut the door behind me, and prayed that no one would break in while I was away. And I ran to the waiting cab with my backpack. The young driver held a Big Gulp out his window, seeming to not care about the rain, and looked me up and down. I quickly showed him my two twenties, and he said his name was D.J. and told me to get in the back.

Mom hadn't come home that Thursday, and *Oum* Palla and Nahrin and I were supposed to meet her at the temple in the evening. As we were putting on our shoes, I told *Oum* Palla that I wasn't feeling well, and she said that I might be coming down with a cold and instructed me to go to bed early.

The taxi smelled like a new car, a scent I attributed to the bowling-pin-shaped freshener hanging from the rear-view mirror.

"Where do you want to go?" D.J. asked me.

I gave him my great-uncle's address. He pushed a couple of buttons on the meter, and we headed down the street. The rain had slowed down to a drizzle, and out in the distance horizontal lines of grays and oranges streaked the early evening sky.

D.J. looked at me in the rearview mirror. "You're not from around here, are you?"

"What makes you say that?"

"Because no young chick like you rides a taxi."

"There's a first time for everything," I said.

"So, where am I taking you? Your boyfriend's?" He raised his left eyebrow at me, and I turned away from the mirror.

When I first saw him, D.J. had seemed like a harmless Big Gulp drinker. But now he was giving me the heebie-jeebies. "No," I said. "I'm going to my uncle's. He's a cop."

D.J. drove us to a neighborhood of old houses. The small street was packed with cars, and several old bikes lay in the driveways. The incessant rain grayed everything around me. A young couple sat on their front porch and watched as we drove by. D.J. stopped for a long time in front of a house with an empty garbage can out on the curb.

"If you want to sit in here, I'll have to charge you."

"Oh," I said, realizing that I was where I had wanted to be. I paid D.J., and he asked if he should come back for me.

Figuring that my uncle would give me a ride back, I said, "No, I'll be fine."

I grabbed my umbrella, got out, and stood on the sidewalk, studying the little house that my father might have lived in when he was growing up. A crooked, short barbed-wire fence circled it, and the grass inside seemed not to have been cut in a very long time. The paint on the windowsill was peeling off, and I couldn't tell what color it had been. I saw the brightness of the TV from inside; faintly I heard a commercial for a used-car dealership. Paper bags full of cans and bottles rested along one wall of the small front porch, which made me think about the cans *Oum* Palla had recycled and the bed she'd bought with the money from it. Then I saw my father. I saw him standing on the porch, looking out at me. Longingly waving at me. "Come here, come here, Gracie. I've been waiting for you forever. Come here and let me hold you," he said.

I ran up to the porch and pressed the doorbell. No one answered. I pressed it again and again. Still no one answered. I knocked on the door. *Boom, boom, boom.*

The door finally opened. And I felt my legs grow light.

He was so old. My father's uncle looked so old. Although I knew that, like Grandma, he wasn't.

I *chumreap suor*-ed him.

Great-uncle Son rested the right side of his body against the door, raising a beer can to his lips. His black hair was disheveled and oily. His chest was thin, the dark reddish-brown skin sagging. Each time he breathed out, I could smell something bitter coming from inside of him.

"What you want?" he slurred in Cambodian. "What is your business?"

"I—" I said, and stopped. I peeked into his dark home. There was a worn recliner sitting just a couple of feet from the television, which was turned on. The house felt too warm and smelled so old.

Uncle Son wobbled back and squinted at me. "What did you say?"

"Do you know Lee Hang?" I asked.

He immediately closed his eyes, squeezing them so tight there were wrinkles on his eyelids, and when he opened them again he raised his beer can at me and cried, "Two people. Now only one." He threw the can into a bag on the porch and showed me his index finger. "I carried him here to America. Do you know that? He broke his leg, and I carried him through the rivers and the mines. I almost died because of him. But I carried him. I carried him. Two of us. And now only one." Then he fell against the door again.

I stepped back, rubbing my arms for warmth, and wondered if I shouldn't have sent D.J. away. As Uncle Son continued to breathe over my head, I wanted to run and pretend that I had the wrong house. Pretend to not know that my father's childhood had been spent in a smelly home with beer cans lying around. But as I looked at the pain on the face of the dirty man standing before me, I realized that this was the person who had brought my father to America, and for this I couldn't be ashamed or scared.

"I am his daughter," I said.

At first my great-uncle seemed unsure of what I had

said, and I didn't explain anything further. I had thought that he would ask me questions like on *Law & Order:* who, what, when, where, and how. But he didn't, and for a long time he stood studying me before he finally asked me inside. As I followed him into the house, I noticed that he was limping, and that stitches ran down the side of his left leg.

I sat on the carpet, next to a pile of old mail and circulars. Uncle Son brought me a mug of tepid water, and then he went to sit in his recliner.

"Is that my father?" I asked, and pointed to a picture hanging above his television.

"No. Seeing his face makes me so sad. Everything is in there." He pointed to an old album lying on top of the Yellow Pages on a small corner table. I went to get it and sat down with it.

I flipped each page of the album slowly. The youngest photo I saw of my father was when he was about ten or so. He was shirtless on the beach, among many young boys, all trying to get in the picture.

With difficulty my great-uncle wobbled to sit beside me, and took half of the album. His arm touched me, and I slowly inched away.

"This. This was a couple of months before the unlucky accident," he said in Cambodian. Even though he hadn't spoken clearly all afternoon, I heard a crack in his voice as he tried to recount the drowning. My father and his friends were clamming. He had gone far out in the ocean, and he stayed there by himself when his friends came back to shore. By the time they went to look for him, he was gone. His body was found later that night, when the moon was out. "He had *bouhn.* He didn't suffer."

I nodded, wanting to believe him. "Did he have a big funeral?"

He nodded.

I took the album back from him. My dad was so young looking. So very young, with a thin face and thick hair. His smile was crooked, and one of his eyes seemed to be sleepy. The collar of his shirt was flipped up, and the short sleeves were rolled up. Maybe one day, if he had lived, he would have grown into the wise and strong man I had thought he would be. But in the picture, he looked as young as some of the boys at my school.

"What was he like?" I asked.

My great-uncle rested his head against the wall and thought about my question. "He was a typical kid. No problem."

"Was my dad funny?"

"Yeah, he was funny."

Like how? "Did he like to talk?"

"No, he talked normal," Uncle Son said.

"What about his parents? Other family members?"

"Everyone died in Cambodia."

I asked quietly, "Was my dad smart?"

For the first time that evening, my great-uncle beamed, and I saw his pretty white teeth as he grinned. "Sure. Your father fixed radios. Once, he fixed a radio in ten minutes." He quickly moved his fingers around, pretending that a piece of equipment was in front him, and then I noticed his pinkies. They were brown and straight. "And he liked to play soccer."

"Really? What position did he play?"

Just like that, Uncle Son fell back into his slump, weighing my question, seeming as though his mind was a maze that he had to find his way out of. "I don't know," he finally said. "He kicked around the ball."

"Did he have a lot of friends?"

With some annoyance my great-uncle said, "Sure. He was a kid." Then he got up, limped back to his recliner, and fell into it. He didn't seem to know that I was still nearby.

As I watched my great-uncle stare at the television screen, I didn't think he was watching or listening to it. I thought the television was just something that gave noise to his life. And even though staying would not gain me anything more, I didn't want to go. Not yet. And I couldn't determine why, except that it wasn't enough. My great-uncle, my father's picture, the house my father grew up in. These were the things that I'd wanted. And they hadn't been enough.

A little later I stood up, but Uncle Son didn't seem to notice. He hadn't been ready today for my visit. Maybe another day. But not today. So it was time for me to go. I knew this.

I was at the door when my father's uncle offered me his photo album. He didn't look at me as he said this, but at the television. And as much as I wanted it, I thought that he needed it more than I. I did, however, accept the picture of my father with the crooked smile and place it safely in my backpack.

Outside, I stood near the garbage can, the rain pricking me lightly on the head. The early night was gray and silvery, and the rain made me cold and itchy. I had forgotten my umbrella, and I had also forgotten to call for a taxi. I remembered seeing a gas station not too far from where I was standing, though, and I began to walk.

I hit the corner, just a block from the Chevron station, when a familiar car pulled up to me. I held my head up high, pushed back my shoulders, and stared at it. Mom rolled down her window and told me to get in.

I noticed that Mom was not driving in the direction of *Oum* Palla's house, but I did not say anything. She turned the heat on high for me and handed me napkins. I stared out my window, so grateful to be in Chet's car, to be going so fast, seeing gas stations and light poles passing by, to be warm and safe and not feeling exhaustion from having to walk all the way home. How, I wondered, could my life be this easy when other people's—like my grandmother's and great-uncle's—weren't?

"I would have brought you. What you did was dangerous," Mom said sternly. "Coming to meet someone you'd never seen before."

The sound of her voice hurt my ears, and I cringed at her thinking she knew everything. "He's my family. He's all I've got left."

She pulled into a neighborhood of houses with bumpy brick lanes and parked under a lit lamppost. "I am your mother. You have me."

I snorted. "You don't even like me."

"What are you talking about?"

Her stunned face surprised me. "You should know," I said. "What? Have you forgotten all of your talks about being free? Isn't this why you brought Grandma here, to be free of her—to wash your hands of the past—so that you can fly away and go back to your students? I bet if you could do it all over again, you wouldn't, Mom. You wouldn't go with my dad that night. Just so you would be free of me, too." And I stared out my window again.

"There are things that you will never understand. Not everything is about you."

I moved in my seat so that I could see her fully. The light from the lamppost made her face blue and yellow. "Because they are about you."

"Grace, you are getting out of line."

For a long while she and I sat motionless, breathing the air we were forced to share. I saw myself in the cars that drove past us, and now I was beginning to tire just from thinking about where they'd come from and the many miles they had left before they reached where they wanted to go. I felt sort of numb—I couldn't feel the weight of my legs or my arms or anything else, except for the throbbing in my chest. I wanted to crawl to the backseat, curl into a ball, and just sleep.

Mom pointed to a brown house across from us and said, "Look at that one. That's where I grew up. Except when I was here, those trees were much shorter. Now they're like oversized blooming onions." The house had a big front porch with small steps leading up to it, and two windows, one on either side of the door, facing our direction. A bush of some sort grew along the walls of the house, and up front, three tall trees flanked the road.

She pointed to the window on the right. "I had a princess room. You should have seen it. I had a bed with a white headboard and white matching furniture. My bedspread had blue and purple flowers."

She stopped speaking. Before, I would have asked, pleaded, for her to continue, as if what she was feeding me would never quench my hunger. But now I didn't want to beg her to give me what was mine.

"You know . . . ," my mother said quietly. I looked at her, atonished that she had more to tell me, at her will. "I don't want you to think I had a bad childhood. Your grandma was the one who had a hard life. I don't think I would have been able to go through all that she did." She was almost whispering, and her bare voice made me shiver—not from fright, but from the way it fell on me like a thin layer of unfamiliar clothes.

Her hands were wrapped around the steering wheel, her eyes intent on what was in front of us. And even though I could feel my heart pumping and my head going light from what I was about to hear, I asked, "What happened to Grandma's face?"

My mother sighed and shook her head slowly. "You sure you want to know?"

"Yes," I answered firmly.

"I wasn't there, Grace, so I didn't see what happened. And your grandma never told me. I'd only heard her speak about it once, to *Oum* Palla, in the refugee camp in

Thailand. Every time I asked about it, to get her to talk so that she wouldn't get so scared of fires, she would either turn very, very quiet or she would start screaming.

"At one time during Pol Pot, your grandma was responsible for cooking rice porridge and feeding it to her commune. We were fed very little. A small bowl of mostly water and a couple morsels of rice, once a day. Imagine how hard that was. Not the task itself. But the cooking of it, the smell of the sweet rice bursting in the pot, and not being able to eat it. One day your grandma was stirring the porridge. I don't know, maybe she was hungrier than usual. Or maybe she just wanted to take a chance. Whatever the reason, she ate from the pot. Not a lot. Not even a spoonful. Just a sip from the ladle. And as soon as the broth touched her mouth, a Khmer Rouge walked by. He began hollering at your grandmother. She was frightened, but she couldn't do anything. She couldn't run because if she got caught she would have been killed, and she couldn't even try to fight back. So she just stood there. The Khmer Rouge called over a cadre of his, and the two of them picked up the large pot of porridge off the flames. And with a quick motion, they threw the hot porridge at your grandma. She was able to step back from it in time, but some of the porridge still got to her face. It was so hot that—"

My mother looked out her window at the blue-black sky and gulped down a fistful of air. But she did not finish her sentence. And who needed her to?

I felt the gnawing ache in my throat, and I squeezed my eyes shut, but felt the hotness of my tears anyway. I didn't want to cry! I didn't think I had a right to cry, not when my grandmother hadn't. It seemed that every creature on this planet had to fight to survive. I thought about my great-uncle carrying my father across a minefield, running away from death, and running to a new life, a life that was cut in half in the end; and my grandmother's dead husband and her baby. Oh, her dead baby girl with the fingers and toes! And her burn, too. The pain she must have gone through. Yet she kept on fighting, up to the end.

15

When Mom and I got home, *Oum* Palla and her sons were waiting for us at the dining table. My mother told everyone I was all right and put her hand on my shoulder. I moved away from her touch and excused myself and went to our bedroom, where I lay down on the floor and fell asleep. In the middle of the night, I woke up and went to the kitchen for a glass of water and heard the TV, so I walked into the sunroom and apologized to Chet for breaking my promise. Then I returned to the guest room to sleep on the floor. Three times my mother told me to get in bed. But I didn't, even though I wasn't mad at her.

I couldn't shake it off. The scalding porridge cooking my grandmother's flesh. My great-uncle maneuvering through the minefields. My father struggling in the water. None of it. I hadn't expected to carry these images with me into my future. It was too heavy.

The next afternoon, after the bittermelons and *trei khar* were finished cooking in oversized steel pots, we loaded up Nahrin's and Chet's cars with the items we had bought a couple of days earlier. "Hurry, hurry. We have to greet the monks," *Oum* Palla had said. "And we have to get back for Maly's wedding." I chose to ride with *Oum* Palla and Chet, and we drove behind Nahrin and Mom.

The rain had ceased, but the temple's parking area was muddy. Mom jumped out of the car as soon as Nahrin parked, and ran to the trunk, where she eagerly handed bags to each of us.

Oum Palla and I stayed inside the temple while Mom, Nahrin, and Chet returned to the cars for the rest of the bags. In the large open room, *Oum* Palla pointed to colorful eight-by-ten posters that had been recently hung on the white, newly painted walls. "You see, Grace, each picture tells a story about the human life, which has four parts. There are birth, old age, sickness, and death." I wanted to ask where happiness existed in the span of a human life. "Look at this one," she said. The first poster showed a baby in the center with beautiful young dancers around him.

I was studying the baby when a monk wearing black-rimmed glasses approached us, and I stared at him until *Oum* Palla got on her knees and pulled me down as well. We sat with our legs folded back on the tile floor and bowed three times to him. Moments later a few more monks came to the front room, and we bowed to them as well. I'd never seen monks up close before. Except for their robes, they didn't look anything like Buddha. But what I had heard about them was true: they were bald, even the youngest of them all, who might have been in his early twenties.

All five monks wore orange robes that reminded me of togas. They moved to one wall, where pillows that my mother had helped to sew awaited them, and sat Indian-style side by side on the pillows.

Mom had given *Oum* Palla a photograph of Grandma, and *Oum* Palla had gotten it enlarged and arranged it with a cup of incense sticks on a small, low table while her sons and Mom brought in the remaining bags and placed them in the center of the room, near Grandma's table. My grandmother faced the large open space, and as I looked at her looking out at us, I prayed silently that she was not too hungry.

The oldest monk, who seemed to be the leader of the group, walked over to the bags. He pulled aside the box of white candles that *Oum* Palla and I had worked on and turned around to my mother and me. He asked her if I was her only child. She answered yes, and touched me on the back.

"Do you speak Khmer?" he asked me in Cambodian.

"*Chas*," I answered quietly.

"What is your name?"

"Grace."

"Grr-race?" He held a pen to his chin as he thought it over. "It's a strong name."

I nodded politely and thanked him.

"Your family has been very generous. Do you know what these things are for?" He pointed to the boxes of noodles, sacks of rice, and bags of blankets and towels.

"No," I said quietly.

"*Tweu bouhn,*" he said. "That is doing good deeds for the dead, for someone living, and for yourself. What you're doing now is donating these things to the temple, and everything in this temple is for everyone to use. You're doing something good on behalf of your grandmother. The journey to her next life might be difficult, so we want to help her. It might be cold, and that's why there is a blanket. She might get hungry, so that's why there are rice and fish. It's always good to *tweu bouhn*. Do you understand?"

I had been here for almost a week, but I was still unsure whether I understood the monk. I surveyed the purchases. The blankets, the toilet paper, the packets of noodles. Did a dead person really need these things to be full in the stomach, or to be free as Mom had talked about, before she could be happy with her new life? Wouldn't all of these items just weigh her down on the trip?

I politely nodded at the head monk and thanked him again.

Oum Palla and Mom spoke with the monks about the funeral service on Sunday. Only a few families were left to be called, and the youngest monk offered to do that. The arrangement to leave my grandmother's ashes was formally made with the head monk. Guests would bring more food to the service, and all the plates and silverware had been unloaded and shelved for use. Before we left, the monks reassured Mom that many people would come on Sunday, filling up the entire temple; and she glowed all during the ride home.

❊ ❊ ❊

Later, as we prepared for Maly's wedding, Mom told me to wear my capris and a button-down shirt so as to not mess up my hair. She was wearing a pair of beige pants and a periwinkle twinset, and Nahrin and Chet were dressed in dark slacks and white dress shirts. *Oum* Palla had already left to *Yeay* Mao's house to help with the food, and the brothers said that normally they wouldn't be going over until much later because they liked to make grand entrances. But because of me, they would go earlier than usual. I didn't want to be around anyone, and I no longer cared about wearing flowers in my hair. But I didn't want to break my promise to Maly. I had only two and half more days to go, and then I would be safe back home.

Nahrin parked behind a silver Accord with a stuffed cat in the back window. "Okay, no more laughing for the rest of the night. Be stiff and proper, so that we can fit in."

"Yeah," Chet agreed. "Where you from?" he asked, trying to sound like David's mom. "Where your mom? Huh? What you say? Huh?" He poked me on the arm.

Nahrin laughed so hard that the only way for him to control himself was to hit the steering wheel. Mom pulled an *Oum* Palla and said that he was rude. "Not everyone can speak perfect English like you and your brother," she said.

Maly's dad opened the front door for us. Although it was still early, there was already a lot of excitement in the house. Red and pink streamers hung from the top of each wall, and red balloons dotted them about every two feet. Cambodian music was blasting somewhere, but it was outdone by even more deafening voices and the clattering of pots and knives from the back of the house.

The four of us followed Maly's dad inside, and we greeted everyone we saw, including two suited men sitting against a wall in the dining room, who tipped their chins at us. Maly's dad introduced them as David's brothers.

The dining table had been removed, and in its place and in the living rooms lay colorful plastic straw mats the size of area rugs. A couple of young kids ran back and forth.

We heard *Oum* Palla's voice, and we followed it as though it were the beacon of light pulling us to dock during a storm.

Oum Palla, who still wore working clothes, and about seven other women—some older and some about Mom's age—were in the kitchen, sitting on old sheets on the floor, busily cutting up vegetables and shredding cooked chicken breasts and speaking in Cambodian. David's mom stood at one end of the counter stirring a brown sauce in a large bowl, and *Yeay* Mao walked back and forth between the kitchen and the back room with a big ladle in her right hand. After we *chumreap suor*-ed all the women, Nahrin and Chet joined a couple of other young men out on the patio, and Mom sat down to help. I stood next to the refrigerator, unsure of what to do.

An older woman pointed to Mom and asked *Oum* Palla, "Is that really Naree's daughter?"

"Of course," Mom answered in a friendly tone. "I remember you, *Oum*. Don't you remember me?" The older

247

woman chuckled and talked about how loss of memory came naturally with old age.

Oum Palla pointed to me and said to her, "And that's her granddaughter."

The older woman looked at me. "When did your grandmother pass away?" she asked. I noticed David's mom glancing at me.

"Three weeks ago," I answered quietly.

The older woman tsk-tsked in sympathy. "You never know when you will die," she told her friends, and they all agreed with her.

The kitchen was warm, but I doubted it had anything to do with the stove. I thought it had to do with this understanding among all of these women, the way their fingers rinsed the white bean sprouts in the colander, the way they brushed hair off each other's faces with their elbows, and the language. It was fluid, like the water running out of the faucet. No one interrupted to ask for repetition or translation. This had to be why Grandma had wanted to return to St. Pete.

Another woman said to Mom, "It's good of you to *tweu bouhn* for your mother." And she added in English, "So good."

"Oh, yes," a younger woman agreed. Her thin hair was done in a French braid. "I just went to a funeral up north for the father of one of my cousins. So many people came. The procession was so long. His funeral was so big that five cops on motorcycles directed traffic."

"Five cops?" someone asked. "That's big."

"Yes," another person agreed. "He has a lot of *bouhn*."

"I went to a funeral—" one of the older women began to say, when David's mom cut her off.

"Stop, stop it," she said in Cambodian. "It's my son's wedding. Do you want him to have bad luck? Talking about such sad, unhappy things?"

"Of course not," the older woman said, and chuckled again. "I'm old now. Sometimes that's all I think about." The rest of the women laughed with her, but stopped talking about deaths and funerals.

"*Oum*," I said.

Oum Palla glanced up from her bowl of chicken breasts. "What, *Coan*?"

"Where is *Bang* Maly?"

Many of the women told me that Maly and all her bridesmaids were upstairs getting ready.

Not wanting Maly to start looking for me, I quickly turned around to find her, when David's mom called for me. "Come here," she ordered. I went to her, and she pointed to green onions. There were about a hundred of them, washed, and draining in two colanders. "You cut, like this," she instructed as she took about five stalks and began chopping them into tiny ringlets.

I glanced at the clock on the microwave. "*Chas*," I said uncertainly.

"When you finish, find me. I give you more work," she said, and went away.

Mom looked up at me from the floor, and her face told me she was as perplexed as I was.

I was a third of the way through with the green onions when the women on the floor advised *Yeay* Mao and

David's mom to go change. Guests would begin to come soon. The high pile of chopped green onions in the white bowl in front of me glistened like wet grass. And I continued to chop more of them, my hands getting slippery from the juice of the onions, when the doorbell began to buzz.

Mom and *Oum* Palla were busy with last-minute items: cutting up cilantro, finding extra salt and pepper, MSG, carrots, egg roll wrappers. "Where did that grandma keep her ear rat?" one lady asked in Cambodian as she searched for dried mushrooms. Another lady wanted to know if anyone had checked on the rice porridge in the back. No one had, and they began to scream, sure that it was burning at this moment. Two of them ran to the back, and the older lady calmly stated that if the porridge was burning we would have smelled it by now.

The guests walked into the kitchen, wearing pants or long, pretty *phamourng*, greeting one another and asking if they could help. They were told no.

When I was finally done with the green onions, I searched around for Mom and *Oum* Palla. They were not in the kitchen, and I didn't know where they might have gone. As I stepped around the island, several new women who had recently entered the crowded area glanced at me, and as I walked away, I heard whispers about who I was. Some of them couldn't believe I was Naree's granddaughter, and some of them couldn't believe that Chandra had a daughter. Then I heard: "Who's her father?"

I was certain that Maly must have been wondering where I was by now as I made my way through the crowds of people sitting on straw mats, holding plastic cups. I climbed the staircase that was decorated with red and pink streamers and red balloons. Two kids about three years old were playing peekaboo with their mothers through the stair posts.

Halfway up the stairs, I saw David's mom coming down. She'd changed into a beautiful green *phamourng*. "I'm done with the onions," I said. With a steely face, and before I could say anything else, she took my upper arm, forcing me around, and we descended the stairs. For such a petite woman, her hand held on to me tightly, and I followed her as though I was in trouble.

I said to David's mom, "I need to go get ready. *Bang* Maly's waiting for me. I don't want her to worry."

"Not for you," she said.

"But I have to go change."

"No, you go play," she hissed in English, then smiled as though she'd just remembered to. "No come back here."

She led me to the kitchen, where we saw *Oum* Palla, who had changed into a blue *phamourng*. Then David's mom left me like I was a lost pet whose owner she had found. The kitchen was beginning to empty of people, and for this I was grateful. *Oum* Palla stood at the island and put down her knife carefully. She'd been mincing garlic.

"I need to go change." I tried to catch all feelings in my voice before they came out and exposed how much I wanted to cry. "I have to go change, and *Bang* David's mom won't let me."

"I know," *Oum* Palla said quietly. I didn't know why she was acting so guilty.

I held on to the kitchen island. "Why?"

She didn't answer but instead told me, "It's all right. Don't worry about it."

I swallowed hard and counted the seconds before I asked *Oum* Palla where my mother was.

She didn't know.

I began to walk away, but as I was about to make it out of the kitchen, I turned back around. A couple of people were watching me, but I didn't care. *Oum* Palla's face had drained of any levity it had had, and I knew then. I knew that something was wrong. My mother was husbandless. And so was my grandmother. My great-grandmother, too, after she left my great-grandfather. Finally I understood why David's parents had insisted on meeting me and asking me those questions about my family. I was going to face what it was that they deemed so important for me to face.

"Is it because my dad is dead?" I asked.

"It's just a wedding," she said. Her lack of an answer told me what I wanted to know.

"Was my grandmother in your wedding?" I asked.

"No," *Oum* Palla said. She also said, "Sorry," but I didn't wait for an explanation. I didn't want to hear the excuse why she and her parents couldn't put my grandmother in her wedding, if there was even one. Maybe there wasn't. Maybe it was one of those things that Mom had talked about, a "right" thing being done because that was what had been done, what had been told to you.

I made my way through the crowd of guests again, but this time I went in a different direction. Chet saw me and asked if I was okay. I would have answered him if I knew. I walked out to the backyard.

Kids much younger than I were running around in the yard, using the fruit trees as part of their obstacle course. I walked over to a woman sitting on a low stool beside a garden hose. She had a large tray of chicken wings before her, and she was washing each one carefully. Her hair was frizzy and curly. She didn't seem to mind my presence. Soon, though, she was done with the wings, got up, and left me.

I sat by myself for a while, spraying water on my feet, the only part of me that felt cool and light, and listening to Cambodian music and men's raucous laughter, before I walked to the other side of the house. Just as I rounded the corner, I heard voices, and stopped immediately. They were the voices of Mom and Maly, and they were both angry.

"You know, I'm not surprised that you didn't have the backbone to stand up to your mom, Maly," Mom said. "But I am surprised that you didn't have the decency to call and tell me that my daughter couldn't be in your damn wedding. You could have done that. But you didn't. You could have just come out with the truth instead of making her find out about it like this. What were you thinking? My God, Maly, she's a kid."

"It wasn't my mom's choice," Maly wailed. "It was David's mom." And more calmly she said, "You know, she even had some man look into David's and my birthdates to see what month and day to get married. She doesn't want a bad omen."

"Why? Why do people still hold on to stupid ideas like that?" Mom yelled. "You're punishing my daughter because her mother and grandmother don't have husbands. Do you know how absurd that is?" Maly didn't answer her. "Jeez, I didn't even want Grace to be your bridesmaid. But no, you and your mom pushed it and got her all excited, and then you hung her out to dry, Maly. You're—"

"Are you still upset about my brother's wedding?" Maly yelled back. "Well, if you are, I'm sorry, Chandra. I'm sorry you couldn't be in it, but I had nothing to do with that."

"Of course you didn't," Mom said sarcastically. "No one takes responsibility for anything. Your mother and my mother grew up together, Maly. She should have—"

"Stop being a know-it-all," Maly hollered. "Not all of us can be like you. You leave this place. Make it okay. And then you come back here, walking around like you're better than me. Like even without your mother, you'll be okay. Like I can't be the same way. But you're not better than me, Chandra. You could have trusted me, you know. I know what happened. No—no one told me! I knew right after you left. Everyone knew! I mean, why else would a single old lady and her young daughter leave suddenly? Didn't you think we would be smart enough to know?"

When Mom didn't respond, I tiptoed around the corner, careful not to step on any leaves or twigs. Maly had her back to me and didn't know that I was behind her. Her hair was done in a French twist, and pearls were dotted along it. She wore a robe, so I couldn't see what was underneath it.

"So don't judge me," Maly said, and turned around

abruptly, walking away, bumping into me and not saying anything, as though she hadn't seen me.

Mom didn't notice me at first, either. She had her face turned to a low shrub, and she seemed to be studying each of its leaves. I stood where I was, watching her. Her hand seemed to ache to reach out to the leaves, to touch them individually and see how real and perfect they were. I knew that feeling well. I moved my left foot, and she heard me, looking up.

"Oh, Grace," my mother said, her face lovelier than it had ever been. "I'm so sorry."

Even though her arms weren't open, I ran to her and hugged her. I hugged her because she was all that I had right then. My father was gone and my grandmother was gone, truly gone, and I was in a body of cold water and all I wanted was warmth.

Mom pulled her arms out from under me and held me as though she was shielding me from all the evils in our world. I was pressed so hard against her that I could feel the warmth of her stomach.

"Let's go home," I said.

Mom stood up and pulled me to the side of the house. "Oh, no. We're not going home, not yet."

"But it's so embarrassing. They don't want me."

Mom looked into my eyes, but I wasn't frightened by their sternness. If anything, she seemed relaxed, not at all like someone who had just come from a fight with a friend from long ago. "Grace, I told you this from the beginning. We didn't come here for a wedding or for anything else. We came here for your grandma's funeral. Now, after you dry your eyes, you and I will go inside and we'll sit through tonight's ceremony. And tomorrow we will come back for the rest of the wedding, and tomorrow night we will go to the reception. You and I will eat, and we'll dance. We will not let anyone think they rejected you. Because no one can reject you. You are perfect, Grace. Do you understand that?"

"But they did," I said. "Just like they did with you and Grandma. She took you and ran because of them."

"Maybe." Mom briefly looked up at the heavens. "She didn't run from them, though. She ran to our future. I used to think that your grandmother liked looking at her burn. I couldn't understand why she wouldn't have wanted it removed. I thought she believed her friends over me. I thought the burn was something she used to explain why her life was so sad and unfortunate: why her husband died, even why her daughter got knocked up, why she had to take her daughter and run away from her friends because of it. And maybe she did." Mom's voice faltered. "But I don't think that that is the only reason. You know, it can't be. I think that the scar reminded your grandma of what she had gone through to get here. How far she'd come. How far she could go. Do you know what I mean? Maybe it was also her badge of accomplishment. For all the things that she had done—whether they were right or wrong—for her family. Don't you think?"

I wrapped my arms around my mother's waist, and I cried into her neck, letting my body heave. I pictured my grandmother carrying her off the plane when they landed in the New World, and I thought about their lives before and after that day. My grandmother had not lost to her father's act on that rainy night from long ago. If anything, she had come out of it victorious. Despite her scars and wounds, my grandmother had strength and courage enough to believe that they would make it. And she'd fought to keep that belief alive.

I could faintly hear the monks chanting. The wedding ceremony had started. I wiped my nose and eyes. Mom turned on the water spigot nearby and cleaned my face. She brushed back my hair with her wet fingers and straightened my shirt. I knew that I looked a mess, but my mother didn't seem to care. And when we returned to Maly's wedding, the night had fully set in, with a silver moon.

I couldn't see the bridesmaids very well because Mom and I were standing in the back. Most of the space on the floor had already been taken. Sitting against one wall were the five monks, and even though it was supposed to be a festive occasion, they all appeared very grave. Everyone in the wedding was beautiful. The bridemaids wore varied shades of pink *phamourng*, with white lace tops, and their hair was pinned up with silk flowers. But as beautiful as they were, they didn't compare to their bride, who sat beside her groom in front of the *a-chah*. He was the officiant of the ceremony, and he spoke about marriage.

Once or twice *Yeay* Mao and *Oum* Palla glanced at me, and I didn't know what to do except look away. Although I was no longer embarrassed by having been rejected as a bridesmaid, I was embarrassed for them. They had held on to a superstition that they might or might not have believed in, and in doing it they had turned their backs on my grandmother. But as much as I wanted to, I couldn't blame them for this. I was sure that they had been thinking of their children all the while.

After the ceremony, all the guests formed circles on the straw mats for a late light dinner. Mom and I went to the kitchen and helped bring out large bowls of rice porridge that had been cooked with chicken and topped with chopped green onions and cilantro. My mother walked with grace while serving Maly's guests. And I imitated her as best as I could.

16

Not many people were there for my grandmother's Cambodian funeral. There were about thirty of us. Several old ladies and men, Maly and David and their parents, *Meing* Huor and her family, some people whom I hadn't met but Mom knew, and my father's uncle, whom my mother had called the night before, were in attendance. A lot of food and bound candles would be left over after the funeral service, but it didn't seem to matter. As we were about to start the service, my mother joked that everyone who wasn't present had drunk too much at Maly's wedding and couldn't get up on time, that even she had had a hard time waking up that morning.

Nahrin, Chet, Mom, and I had not attended Maly's morning wedding ceremony. We had stayed late the night before, sweeping the kitchen and washing the bowls, and none of us, except *Oum* Palla, pushed ourselves to get up.

But we did go to her reception. And Mom was right. We ate and drank; Chet and I sat at our table watching her and Nahrin dance to a couple of songs. That night at dinner Nahrin promised that he would visit us in Scottsville often. As I watched my mother on the dance floor in her black dress and her hair pulled back in a chignon, Chet rubbed my head and told me that I could definitely be in his wedding.

Now, like the old women, Mom and I were dressed in white cotton. *Oum* Palla had taken the material we bought at Jo-Ann Fabrics and cut it and sewed two button-down shirts, two simple long skirts, and two very long scarves that we draped over ourselves like beauty pageant sashes. In our white garb, I felt as though Mom and I were pledging a sorority. She looked as though she would have a good chance of getting in; I did not.

Mom and I sat across from the monks, and all of us brought our hands together under our noses, in prayer form. The monks chanted in unison, and the buzzing rhythm blocked off all other sounds, filling up every corner of the building, every pocket of air, like bees. I couldn't make out a word they were saying—I never could. Once in a while they stopped only to take deep breaths before they continued where they had left off. My mother had been right, their chants did sound like something on Grandma's tapes, and I bathed in it.

Three monks closed their eyes, their heads and bodies still, and all five of them seemed far away from this world as they focused on one nearer their souls. And I closed my eyes, too. I thought about the scrapbook I had thrown away that morning. The window Grandma and I had liked looking out of. The way Mom had held Grandma whenever Grandma was frightened. The sound of my name. My father's young face. My uncle. The plane ride here. The burn, too. And the tiny toes.

When I opened my eyes, the white candles with the baby's breath were being passed around and lit. Mom and I took ours, and the monks chanted some more. Later several of us spoke about my grandmother. Chet shared that no one other than his mother and my grandmother had spanked him, and that my grandmother had spanked harder. Another person said that my grandmother had been a kind woman. *Oum* Palla said that she hoped my grandmother knew we were doing this *bouhn* for her. I said that I would always miss my grandmother. When it was my mother's turn to speak, I felt all eyes on her. She was laughing and crying, wiping her nose a couple of times.

As everyone listened, Mom spoke about the sailboat day. Everyone in the temple was doubling over, some even holding on to their stomachs as my mother described Grandma flinging out her arms like an airplane and flying up and down the sidewalk, singing her rain song.

I laughed with everyone as I remembered my grandmother on that rainy day. But unlike them I remembered, too, the arguments in our kitchen and the sound of my mother's feet tramping up to her room afterward. And I thought I always would. As with everything in the past, what had happened had happened and would never change, no matter how ugly or smelly it was. My grandmother had been ashamed of her daughter—and had done the only thing she could think of to save them both. And my mother—out of spite and hurt—had refused to return to the one place that her mother had felt was closest to home. But no matter how hard it might have seemed, I had to understand these things, and accept them, as I already did, in order to understand where my family was from, and where I was from, and where I was going.

There are people I know who strive for great things in this world. Besides Mom's gifted students, I know of a senior girl at school who traipses from class to class with a planner that tells her what to do each half hour. In addition to school, she has to fit in her daily voice lessons, basketball practice, community work, and private French lessons—taught by a real Frenchman; she's planning on going to Columbia University. There is also the kid who has been on television; he says he wants to be the youngest author with a number-one bestseller. I admire these people and others who are like them. I am not one of them. I will never be able to do what they will do or know what they will know. But I do know this. I know that rice and noodles and soy sauce do not fill a person up and set her free. It is forgiveness and understanding. Forgiveness and understanding can set anyone free, maybe even free enough to fly.

Spirit of Life, come unto me.
Sing in my heart all the stirrings of
        compassion.
Blow in the wind, rise in the sea,
Move in the hand, giving life the shape
        of justice.
Roots hold me close; wings set me free.
Spirit of Life, come to me, come to me.

ABOUT THE AUTHOR

MANY LY and her husband, Danith, live with their dog, Pluto, in Pittsburgh. Many works for Greater Pittsburgh Literacy Council. She likes to spend her free time at home playing with Pluto and writing.